Wanting Mr. Wilde

Wie-aam Adams

Published by Wie-aam Adams, 2024.

WANTING MR. WILDE

First edition. July 23, 2024.

Written by Wie-aam Adams.

To the girl whose eyes I opened to the world of romance and spice.

You're welcome ;)

CHAPTER 1 – TAKARA

"To being single!"

We cheers our drinks before finishing them off in one go.

I'm not even mad that we're cheering to being single and not my birthday. Well, to be fair, it's not my birthday *yet*. Not for another ten minutes. Also, new year's. That's another thing to look forward to in ten minutes. People often ask me how I feel having my birthday on the first day of the year. I merely shrug them off, like I don't care. But I do care. I feel like it's unfair, because people don't celebrate me on my birthday, but rather new year's. I haven't felt appreciated on my birthday for as long as I can remember. Maybe I'm being childish, but just once, I want to be celebrated on *my* birthday.

"Seven more minutes," my best friend, Zoe, says. "Now is the time girls. Find yourselves a hunk of a man and have your first kiss of the year when the fireworks explode."

Our friends disperse, looking for a "hunk" to kiss, whereas I stay behind. Zoe comes to sit next to me, a knowing smile on her face.

"Come on Kara. This could be a big night for you," she says. I look away from her. It could be. It really could be. But do I want it to be? I mean, I guess there is something quite romantic about a new year's kiss, and what better time to just get my first kiss out of the way with no strings attached? Yep, that's right. Not only would it be my first kiss of the year, but it would be my first kiss *ever*. And that's not something to take lightly. If people hear that I've never been kissed before, they call me names. I've been called a prude, conservative, and even a party pooper, for some reason. That's why I don't tell people. It's also the reason why I recently got myself a boyfriend, to shut down any rumours that may have formed throughout my years on high school, and about two hours ago, I broke up with him. It might sound brutal, but since I'm going to college this year, where no one knows me, I don't have any more use for him. Him making a bet that he could take my virginity before the end of the year also made ending things easier.

"I don't know, Zoe," I say, looking back to her.

"Oh, come on," She whines. "Just take a look around, and if there's really no one who piques your interest, I'll let it go. I promise."

Sighing through my mouth, I look away from her and scan over the potential kissing partners in the bar. Not you. Not you. Not you either. Definitely not you.

"Zoe, I hate you break it to you, but there's really no one -"

My heart stops.

There, in the corner of the bar, occupying one of the cream couches, is the most devastatingly handsome man I've ever seen. I can't make out much from all the way over here, but I can make out the mop of jet-black hair on his head, his sharp jawline, and his pale skin. I can also see his long legs underneath the table. Damn, they're long. And thick, too. Not so slender like boys in this day and age.

What did my mom used to say? If the legs look like that, then how does the-no. Stop right there.

"I see you've found yourself a target," Zoe says, following my line of vision.

Yes, I have. There's only one problem though. The blondie on his lap.

I can practically smell the lust radiating from her, and she doesn't bother in hiding it, staring at him with seductive eyes and biting her lip.

It will just be my luck. Being attracted to a man who clearly cannot be mine, at least not tonight. No, tonight, he is hers.

I look away before I become depressed. I can't be depressed, not when it's about to be my birthday. I down a shot, slamming the glass on the table. Then suddenly, I feel confident. Confidence creeps into my body, overtaking all my senses, and before I even realize it, I'm standing up from my seat and straightening out my little black dress that Zoe made me wear.

"Give me your lipstick," I tell Zoe who wordlessly hands it to me. I don't miss the glint in her eyes. She knows what's about to happen.

I drag the dark red lipstick across my lips, using Zoe's tiny mirror to make sure that I didn't mess up. Then I pull my hair out of its ponytail, running my fingers through my natural waves. I've always been told I look older and more mature with my hair down.

And then I'm off in the direction of *him*.

"You go girl!" Zoe cheers on behind me. The closer I get to where he's sitting, the stronger the need for another drink becomes. But no. I'm a lightweight and I cannot afford to be drunk when I'm speaking to this man. I need to be level-headed. Or at least something close to that.

You can do this, Kara. All you have to ask for is one kiss. Just one little kiss. Even just a peck will do. Then he's blondie's for the rest of the night.

I stop at their table. Blondie notices me first, immediately glaring at me.

"What do you want?" she snaps, her face twisting up into something very ugly.

Then he looks up. And right at me. Oh my lord.

My knees buckle.

He's even more breathtaking up close. His eyes, they are a vibrant blue colour, so bright yet so pale at the same time, reminding me of the wild ocean and a delicate snowflake at the same time. And his lips, oh his lips. They're so red, and so plump, and I know he didn't use any product to make it look like that. No, that's all natural. Unlike mine, and blondie's over here.

"Can I help you?' he speaks for the first time, his voice sounding so velvety, and oh my. I think I just peed myself.

Suddenly, I can't speak. All I can do is make weird sounds with my mouth. Where did all that liquid courage go to? I'm suddenly sober all over again.

"Cat got your tongue?" he teases, an amused glint in his so beautiful eyes. It surprises both me and blondie who both look at him with wide eyes. Did he just...was that flirting?

Then he looks at blondie, his expression becoming stoic.

"Get off."

"What?" She blinks in confusion.

"Get off me before I push you off," he says, his demeanour completely changing. She looks like she wants to protest, but upon seeing the look in his eyes, she's scrambling off his lap and away from us.

Swallowing, I start to turn. "I think I need to use the bathroom –"

A hand wrapping around my wrist stops me. I turn back, staring down at his hand around my wrist. It's so big, adorned by a single silver band on his index finger. Then my eyes travel up, to his exposed arm. It's so muscular and veiny.

Then he stands up and my eyes snap up to his. My free hand clenches into a fist at my side. He's so tall, towering over me completely. My head barely reaches his shoulders, and I'm not short, not by long shot. How tall is he? What-6ft5 or something?

"Didn't you come here because you had something to ask me?" he questions, his posture relaxing from when he was talking to blondie.

"Ah. Well...it's...You see..."

Then the lights in the bar go off. No, it can't be midnight yet. I haven't even spoken a single word to him yet, never mind ask him to be my new year's kiss.

"It must be midnight right about now," he speaks. Then suddenly, he lets go of my wrist and an arm wraps around my waist and I'm pulled into his chest.

"What –"

A pair of wet lips meet mine.

I freeze, my eyes widening. Fireworks go off in the background. This is it. I'm officially nineteen. And I'm having my first kiss.

His lips are unbelievably soft, softer than I ever could have imagined them to be.

My eyes slowly flutter closed, and I slowly give in to the nice feeling. He tilts my head slightly, deepening the kiss, and I let him. This is not the peck, or chaste kiss at most I was planning on, but the moment he flicks his tongue against my bottom lip, I decide that I don't care.

This is so much better.

His fingers wrap around the back of my neck, delving into my thick hair that flows there.

Then suddenly, he pulls away, but just a breath away from me.

"Kiss me back, you beautiful thing."

And then he's kissing me again. This time around, I decide not to be scared and let my inexperience show. Slowly, I move my lips with his, parting my lips when he teases them with his tongue. The moment his tongue touches mine, my entire body falters, but luckily, he's there to catch me and hold me up, all against him.

His fingers stroke my face and I grip his shirt in between mine, desperately holding on to him. Becoming bolder, I trail my fingers up his shirt, until I touch skin. He groans into my mouth, giving me the encouragement to continue. I move my hand up to his neck, curling my fingers around his thick neck, feeling the hair there.

This kiss isn't wild. But it's not gentle either. It's sensual. Slow. But that quickly changes.

His hand moves down from my waist and travels down the side of my leg, and a shiver goes through me when he touches skin. Since when was my skin so sensitive? But he stops at the hem of my short dress, not moving any further.

"Can I please touch you?" he breathes against my lips. My eyes open, and that's when I realize that the lights have turned back on.

Panic creeps in and before I even realize it, I'm pushing him away from me, breaking our kiss. He seems startled by my sudden actions, blinking out of a daze of lust. His lips, his cherry lips, are so swollen. I bet mine are too.

"I...I'm sorry." I don't even know what I'm apologizing for. For pushing him away?

He blinks at my apology. Then a small smile appears on his lips. He appears to have snapped out of that daze.

"It's okay," he says, taking a step towards me. "You have nothing to apologize for. You were great."

I was...great? But I barely knew what to do and didn't even kiss him back at the beginning. And that was great for him?

"That's my best friend!" I suddenly hear Zoe cheering from behind me. I jump, startled.

Oh no. Did she see everything? Did the other girls also see? How long have the lights been on for now?

Then suddenly, he's grabbing my hand, bringing my attention back to him.

"Are you okay?" He sounds truly concerned. I must look like a wreck then.

"Can you please get me out of here?"

I don't even know what I'm asking of this man, this complete stranger, but I doubt I can look at Zoe any more than I can look at him, so he seems to be my best bet at getting out of here.

He must sense the plead in my eyes because he quickly nods, and then he's pulling me with him.

Out of the bar.

To who knows where.

CHAPTER 2 – TAKARA

I end up in his car.

I don't know how we went from being complete strangers to us kissing and then me climbing into his car with him. The moment he got me out of the bar should have been when I said goodbye, but instead, when he offered me a ride, saying how taking a taxi at this time of night was dangerous, I said yes. Honestly, I'm not even sure if he's safer than those perverts driving the taxis in the middle of the night. At least he hasn't made any moves on me, not after kissing me back there.

But now we sit in complete silence in his car, his car he hasn't bothered in starting yet despite saying he would drive me home.

"Sorry." I suddenly hear and my head snaps up, my eyes meeting his. Did he say something? Was he speaking this entire time? I was still processing how we got here, to this point.

"No, I'm sorry. What were you saying?" I apologize.

"I was asking where you live. So I can put it in the GPS," he says and I instantly feel embarrassed. Here I was thinking he tricked me while he's been asking for my address all along.

So, to avoid any further embarrassment, I quickly tell him my address and he puts it into the GPS on the screen in his car. Wow, now that I'm really looking at his car, it's so sleek, and new, with leather seats and everything. I don't know much about cars, but I do know that I like this one.

I expect him to start the car now, but instead, he leans over the console and brings his face incredibly close to mine. I freeze, my eyes widening ever so slightly. Having him so close to me reminds me of our kiss, and how I was pressed up against him. My eyes can't help but flutter down to his lips, his cherry lips that seem so inviting right now.

No. I can't be thinking like this. New year's kiss and first kiss is only once. Any more kisses after that is...more. So, why do I want to kiss him again? Is it because he hands down gave me the most perfect first kiss ever? And maybe I want to try again now that I sort of know what to do now?

But then, he's pulling the seatbelt over me and pulling away, clicking it into place. I blink. Once. Twice.

He wasn't trying to kiss me again. He just wanted to fasten my seatbelt because I forgot to do it myself. That was such a cliché move. How did I not recognize it? Dammit. How many times am I going to embarrass myself still? Hopefully no more until I can get home.

"Ready to go?" he asks and I'm about to nod when suddenly, my stomach growls. My eyes widen and my head snaps down, my hand immediately going to my stomach. I then look at him, hoping only I could hear it, but when I see the look on his face and how hard he's trying not to laugh, I realize. He heard.

I offer him a sheepish look.

"Would you like to get some food on the way?" I'm about to say no because I can eat at home, but my stomach answers for me, and apparently, it disagrees with me. He starts the engine. "I'll take that as a yes."

I slump into the soft leather seat, avoiding his eyes. This night cannot possibly get more embarrassing for me.

In no time, he pulls up to my favourite burger joint in town, not only because of the food, but also because it's open 24 hours a day.

"I hope you don't mind," he says, and I immediately shake my head, my lips forming a smile. I'm quick to jump out of the car. Then he speaks again. "Wait."

I listen, standing beside the car while he rounds it, a jacket in his hands. He then wraps the jacket around my waist and ties the arms at the front. I'm confused until I look down and catch a glimpse just before he ties it closed. My legs. When I was in the car, I had completely forgotten about how short the dress truly is. But he clearly noticed. Wait. Does that mean I possibly could have flashed him all throughout the car ride and before then?

How embarrassing.

"You coming?" he asks, already walking ahead of me.

"Coming!" I say, ignoring the embarrassment and joining him. We enter the restaurant and it's empty, to be expected considering the time.

"What do you want? It's on me," he says, gesturing to the big menu. I suddenly feel shy. I always pig out when I come here, but I doubt he'd appreciate seeing that. So I just order a normal cheeseburger and fries, pouting slightly because I know it won't fill me. Then he orders. "Make the burger a double with extra fries plus onion rings and make that two."

My eyes snap to him. Did he just...order me more food?

He must feel the way I'm looking at him because he says, "You look hungry."

My cheeks flush. Was it that obvious?

"Don't worry," he says, leaning in closer. "I like girls who eat well."

Then he grabs my hand and pulls me to a booth in the corner, hidden from the public eye. Coincidence? I don't think so.

Instead of sitting opposite me, he sits down next to me.

And then I realize something, something I should have realized a lot sooner.

"I don't even know your name," I say. He turns to me, a slight smile playing on his lips.

"You first."

O-kay.

"I'm Takara. But you can call me Kara. Everyone does."

"Nice to meet you, Takara," he says. "I'm Avery."

Hot.

"Nice to meet you too," is what I say instead of voicing my thoughts. "Avery."

It tastes delicious on my tongue. I like it.

Our food comes and my mouth waters at all the food. Avery did say he likes girls who eats well, so I'm not going to bother in pretending I'm something I'm not. He eats even faster than me, practically devouring everything in front of him without leaving even a single crumb behind. I'm impressed.

I take the last bite of my burger and sigh in content, unconsciously rubbing my belly.

"Are you satisfied?" he asks.

"More than," I breathe out. I'm not sure I'll be able to walk out of here any time soon. And I'm definitely too heavy for him to carry.

"I'm glad. I aim to satisfy." Somehow, I think he's talking about more than the food.

I immediately think of our kiss, and my entire body flushes. That was one good kiss alright. And I have a feeling he was being gentle. I wonder how it would be if he kissed me rough.

No, I shouldn't wonder about that. Why? Because it's never going to happen.

"Shall we go?" he asks but I shake my head.

"In a minute."

He chuckles but doesn't question me. I have a feeling he knows why.

Then his phone beeps and he takes it out, reading whatever message he just received. Who texts someone at one in the morning? Oh no, could it possibly be his girlfriend? He wouldn't be alone in a bar on New Year's Eve and definitely wouldn't have kissed me if he had a girlfriend. Maybe it's his mom?

I take his distraction by his phone to look at him. Properly. From his thick perfectly trimmed eyebrows to his sharp-edged nose down to his lips that have puckered out in a pout as he focuses. I want to bite that lip. That bottom lip. I should have when I had the chance.

I wonder. What does he think of me? I know how I think of him, but how does he see me? Really.

He must find me attractive on some level to have kissed me.

"You keep staring at me like that and I'm going to have a real problem," he suddenly says, startling me.

"Problem?" I ask.

He turns his head to me, dropping his phone onto the table.

"Yes. Problem."

"What kind of problem?" I ask.

"A problem that would probably make things very awkward for me," is all he says.

What is that supposed to mean?

"If you'll excuse me, I have to use the bathroom." He excuses himself.

What the...? Did I do something wrong?

"Kara?" a familiar voice says.

Oh no.

I look up, my eyes meeting my ex's of exactly three hours.

Damn. I can just not get a break tonight, can I?

"Chris, to what do I owe the pleasure?" I say, plastering the fakest smile I can muster up on my face.

"I was really hoping it wasn't you," he says. "I mean, there's no way you'd already be with another guy so soon after I broke up with you."

I broke up with him, but I'll let him have that considering how abrupt me ending things was. I mean, I didn't even think of his feelings when I did it. Like, who knows? I was with him because he was of use to me, but for all I know, he really had feelings for me. Maybe even still.

"Well, too bad. Because it is me," I say, and then his face becomes dark. Angry.

"How could you?" he exclaims. Luckily, there's no other customers here to see this. "How could you get with the next man who showed a little interest in you after I broke up with you?"

Again, I broke up with him, but who has time for the semantics.

"Did you do things with him? Did you let him touch you?" he questions, his eyes scarily dark.

Yes, but that's not the point.

"What I do and who I do it with is none of your business," I say, surprisingly calmly.

"So he did touch you," he says, his voice dropping. "How could you do that? You didn't even let me hold your hand unless I practically begged you!"

Okay, so maybe I wasn't the most loving girlfriend, but obviously I was trying to send a message. I don't like you.

"Are you done?" I ask.

"No, I'm not done," he says, and then suddenly, he's grabbing me, pulling me up and against him. I immediately fight against him, but his hold is too strong. "You owe me, Takara."

"I don't owe you anything," I say, knowing exactly where this is going. Now I wish we chose to sit at a less secluded table. How did he even see us?

"Yes, you do," he says. "We dated for five months and I didn't even get one kiss. I thought it was maybe because you were shy, so I didn't force you. But now, you let some random guy grope you in public?"

Wait. Avery didn't grope me here. How does he...

"Were you at the bar?" I question and the look in his eyes tells me yes. He was at the bar. He saw everything. He just pretended before to bait me. To see if I'd tell the truth. "Did you follow us here?"

Another yes. I can see it in his eyes.

"Let me go," I say, struggling against him, but this only makes him pull me closer.

"Not without a kiss," he says, leaning forward. Before I know it, I'm slapping him across the face. His head whips to the side, his eyes widening in surprise.

"You're sick." I spit.

How did I not realize he was such a psycho when I was dating him? I mean, we spent five whole months together. How did I not see it?

"You bitch." He snarls and then suddenly, I feel a sting in my right cheek and I'm falling backwards into the booth, knocking the table with my arm in the process. I stare up at him with wide eyes, holding my burning cheek.

He slapped me. He *hit* me.

"You –" He's cut off by someone pulling him back and punching him in the jaw so hard, I hear a crack. He goes flying back, hitting the ground with a loud thud. I look up, my eyes meeting a pair of fiery blue ones.

Avery.

He immediately rushes to me, his hands hovering over my face, as if he's afraid he'll hurt me if he touches me.

"Are you okay? Did you get hurt?" he rushes out, his eyes filled with worry and concern. No one's looked at me like that before. No one's cared enough about me to look at me like this when I have gotten hurt in the past. It makes me feel like he actually cares about me, as absurd as that it.

Tears fill my eyes.

"He hit me." I whimper. Avery immediately pulls me into his arms, his touch much gentler and welcomed than Chris's. He strokes my hair as I bury my face in his neck, sniffling. No one's ever hit me before. Not even my parents when I was a naughty child. So, what gave him the right to lay his hand on me?

I'm both angry and heartbroken.

"Shh. It's okay. He won't hurt you again. I'm here now," he whispers into my hair. And I believe him.

I feel safe.

In his arms.

Safer than I've ever felt before.

CHAPTER 3 – AVERY

This girl is so fragile.

So vulnerable.

That boy, he ex, lays out cold on the floor, blood dripping from his jaw onto the tiles. I feel sorry for the worker who's going to have to clean that up.

After a few minutes, Kara finally stops sniffling and brings her face out of my neck. She's no longer crying, but that heartbroken look lingers in her eyes. I completely understand. Who would ever think someone you dated, maybe even loved, would do such a thing to you?

Her cheek is red, angry.

Anger creeps into my body once more, but I shove it away. If I let it take over me like I did before, that boy will most likely end up dead on that floor.

Instead, I focus on Kara in front of me, who stares at me with such vulnerability it makes my heart clench in my chest. I want to touch her, take her face into my hands and comfort her, but I don't want to hurt her, and judging by the look on her face, she wants the same thing.

"Avery," she whispers, and I feel a twitch in me. In my pants. This reminds me of how she looked at me before I excused myself. Like she was in awe of me. Like she couldn't believe I was real. Like she wanted to touch me. I know I wanted her to. I wanted her hands all over me. My pants become tighter at the mere thought of her hands on me. No, Avery. Now is not the time.

"Yes, baby?" I unconsciously call her by a pet name, and her face turns red. My lips twitch. She's cute.

"I...I can't..." she trails off, hesitating.

"It's okay. Tell me," I say, as gently as I can.

"Instead of dropping me off at home, could you drop me off at a hotel instead?" Somehow, I know that isn't what she wanted to tell me

14

at first, but this is what she decided to go with. "I can't go home looking like this."

She gestures to her cheek.

I understand. But a hotel? Does she have money for that?

"Why don't you come home with me?" The words come flying out of my mouth before I even realize what I said. Her eyes widen, mimicking mine. "You don't have to if you don't want to or don't feel comfortable. I'll just drop you –"

"Yes," she cuts me off. What?

"Yes?" I repeat and she nods.

"Yes. I'll go home with you."

There is still some hesitance in her voice, but her eyes tell me she's certain of her decision. And that's all I need.

So, I grab her hand and we leave the restaurant. I quickly call the ambulance for the boy lying knocked out on the floor before driving to my apartment. I live in a secure complex, well, it's not as much a complex as it is a tall skyscraper of a building with apartments on each floor. I live right at the top, at the penthouse. Kara stares at the building with awe, and then again at my apartment.

"You must be rich to live in a place like this," she blurts out, and then realizes how it sounded. "I'm not a gold-digger or anything. I just meant –"

"I know what you meant," I cut her off, putting her at ease. I don't bother in telling her that this entire building belongs to me, mainly because it's only so because I inherited it from my late father. He was rich. Me? Besides my inheritance? Not so much.

Then, it seems like we both become acutely aware that we're completely alone. Just the two of us. For the first time. I think back to the bar.

How shy she looked when I spoke to her for the first time. How she bit her bottom lip as she contemplated on what to say first. I was intrigued by her. She looked so mature, but her actions and shyness told me she wasn't as old as she looked then. But her being in a bar means she is old enough, and that's all it took for me to send the blonde girl off and focus on her instead. I'm not even sure why I indulged in that blonde girl's advances. Why I let her sit on my lap. Maybe it was because it was New Year's Eve and I had nothing better to do than pick a girl up at a bar and take her home with me. Well, not home home. To a hotel somewhere. I never bring girls to my actual home.

Until now.

So technically, I did bring a girl home with me from the bar, but not for the reasons I had before. With this girl, I don't even know if I'll get to touch her again, never mind bring her to my bed. I'd seduce her, especially since she seems so interested in me, but she's too fragile at the moment, and I'm not some asshole who's going to take advantage of her.

Her phone beeps with messages. But she ignores it, just like she did in the car, saying she'll respond in the morning.

"So...let me take you to the room you'll be sleeping in tonight," I say and she nods, looking down at the ground. I don't know why she won't even look at me right now. Did I maybe do something I'm not aware of?

I lead her to one of the guest bedrooms, the one closest to my bedroom. I try to fool myself by telling myself it's in case she needs something, but I'm way too selfish for that. Does it make me an asshole for hoping that at some point in the night, she'll come knocking on my door and crawl into bed with me? Not for sex, just sleeping. Right now, I'll take anything I can get. As long as I can touch her again. Feel her against me.

"Thank you, Avery," she whispers, so soft I nearly don't catch it. And then she disappears into the bedroom, the door closing behind her. I purse my lips. I didn't even get to offer her anything, like water or something more comfortable to sleep in. I can only imagine how uncomfortable that dress must be. It's so short and tight. I mean, it gives me a great view of her curvy body, but I don't know how she can possibly move around in that.

I nearly lost it when we drove from the bar. She didn't even notice it, but her dress rode up when she sat down, giving me a view of her thick thighs. It's thicker than girls I've been with before, but I loved it. That along with her wide hips and big bust, she was unlike any other girl I've seen before. But that was a good thing. I didn't want her to be like those girls. She was unique in her own way, a way that I appreciated. A lot.

I go to my room, strip out of my clothes down to my boxer briefs and climb into bed. I toss and turn for the next hour. I feel restless, with Kara in the next room. I wonder if she feels the same way. Then, as if she knows I've been thinking about her, I hear a soft knock on my door.

I jump up from the bed, leaping over to the door and pulling it open quickly, afraid that she may walk away. Her eyes show how startled she is.

"Is everything alright?" I ask her.

She's still wearing that skimpy dress but has tossed my jacket. Then she becomes aware of how exposed I am, her eyes traveling down my bare chest to my abs and then the trail of hair that leads into my underpants. Her ears turn red as she looks down at my bulge, but her eyes are wide, like she's fascinated. By it. My package. Like a chain reaction, I twitch in my boxers and her eyes become even wider. She noticed.

Then I take a step forward, placing my hand on her waist. She tenses under my touch, her eyes snapping up to meet mine. She blinks. Once. Twice. She looks nervous, but she doesn't push me away, which I take as a good sign. Then I place my other hand on the other side of her waist and lift her off the ground, causing her to squeal. She instinctively wraps her legs around my waist, and I inhale sharply when her pelvis meets mine.

"Can I get something more comfortable to sleep in, please?" she pipes out. I know this sign. She knows where this was going, and she's putting a stop to it.

Nodding, I set her down at the edge of the bed and walk to my closet. I find an extra-large white shirt and hand it to her. I expect her to leave now, now that she's got what she came here for, but instead, she stands up and starts pulling the dress over her head.

I tense up. What is she doing?

She tosses the dress aside and stands before me in just her undergarments. She looks uncertain, but I can't stop staring at her body. From the way her breasts strain against the red lace bra she wears, down to the dip of her stomach and then to her legs, her fleshy thighs. She can basically be standing completely naked in front of me, yet she's not, but even just like this, with her private parts still covered thoroughly, I'm *hard*. So very hard it's painful.

"Avery," she whispers, her voice throaty.

"Yes, baby?"

"Please touch me."

That's all I need before I'm pouncing on her, forcing her to lay back on the bed as I cover her body with mine.

Ou lips meet in a fiery and passionate kiss, my fingers delving into her thick hair and her legs coming up to wrap around me. She's just as insatiable as I am, kissing me back with such a hunger, I feel myself start to lose control. I grind my lower half against hers, eliciting a moan out of her.

Fuck, I love that sound.

"Let me touch you, please," I murmur, and she nods instantly, spreading her legs further for me.

I dip my hand in between our bodies and caress her through her underwear, our lips parting with a breathless gasp from her. However, just as I use my finger to part the thin lacy fabric to the side, she uses an *impressive* amount of strength and flips us over so that she's now on top and straddling my waist.

"I want to pleasure you."

I groan, throwing my head back at her words. Fuck, she can. She *so* can.

She tugs at the hem of my boxer briefs, staring expectantly at me. I lift my hips, urging her on and she uses this as an opportunity to pull my underwear down my legs, my cock springing free and standing proud against my abdomen, leaking from the head.

She gasps, staring at it with big eyes.

"You're so...big," she whispers in awe, and I smirk, but it's quickly wiped off my face when she wraps her hand around me, a surprised groan escaping me.

"Fuck, I curse out loud, screwing my eyes tightly shut.

She starts moving her hand up and down my shaft, slowly, teasingly.

"Don't tease me, baby," I practically beg like some pre-pubescent teenager whose having his dick touched for the first time. It's strange, because I'm *always* in control and always hold onto my composure, yet this girl who looks like she's never seen a dick before in her life has me losing my mind, and she's *barely* touching me.

She nods, looking determined, but what she does next is the last thing I expect. I expect her to fasten her strokes, but no. This motherfucking crazy girl takes me into her mouth, the warmth of her tongue sending me over the edge, my hips bucking.

I explode in her mouth.

Fuck, that was over way too fast. I usually last much longer. No, I *always* last much longer. It's definitely been too long.

When I open my eyes, I find Kara to be blushing, a shy smile playing on her lips.

"Was that good for you?" she shyly asks. I sit up, grabbing onto her hips to stable her on me.

"Good?" I exclaim in disbelief. "Baby, I nutted so quickly, I should be fucking ashamed of myself, yet you ask me if it was good for me?"

Her smile widens, and that's when I notice the remnants of my cum dripping from her chin.

"You did so well, baby," I say, wiping it away with my thumb. "You even swallowed."

Her blush deepens and I smirk, getting a loud squeal out of her when I suddenly flip us over.

She's had her fun, and now, it's my turn.

CHAPTER 4 – TAKARA

Avery made me pass out from so much pleasure.

I swear, he had me seeing stars and I just couldn't keep myself conscious. Embarrassing, I know.

I'm not sure how long I was passed out.

Maybe just a few seconds. But I'm embarrassed, nonetheless. How could I have passed out after what we...what we just did?

What happened to me? I don't regret what we just did, but I'm shocked at how bold and confident I was. And it had nothing to do with liquid courage. It was all me.

I look at my hand. I touched his...I touched someone's penis for the first time. The skin was soft but the penis itself was hard. Very hard. At one point, I was afraid that I might hurt him, but when he kept moaning and groaning, I realized that he liked it. A lot. And that just spurred me on.

And he...he kissed me...down there. He licked and sucked too. I cover my face with my hands. I should be embarrassed by the sounds I made. I didn't even shave. He didn't seem to mind though. Oh my God, he saw me. My most private part, he saw. And he put his mouth there.

How did I go from not even having my first kiss to ending up almost completely naked in bed with a man I didn't know before tonight? I don't know if I should feel proud or ashamed. Zoe would be proud of me, I know.

Speaking of Zoe, she has blown my phone up with messages that I should probably reply to. I will. Later. Later when I'm not naked from the waist down.

Avery returns to the room with a white cloth in his hand. He crawls back in between my legs, pushing them open and wiping me. The cloth is warm on my skin, and I'm surprised I'm not pushing him away. But then again, why should I, when he's already seen me there?

"You okay?" he asks when he's done cleaning me up. I nod, pulling my legs closed again. He smiles at my action before grabbing onto my ankles and pulling me forward towards him. I squeal in surprise, grabbing onto his shoulders. He reaches behind me and pulls open the covers.

Then he places his hand on my face, on my cheek where I was slapped and soothes it with his cold fingers. He leans forward, placing the gentlest kiss to my lips, my eyes fluttering closed.

"Sleep," he says. My eyes open. "I'm going to take a shower."

Then he stands up and disappears into the en-suite bathroom. I soon hear the sound of the shower turning on and the water running. I can only imagine him standing under that shower, stark naked, letting the water caress every inch of him.

Shaking my head, I crawl under the covers and lay my head down on a pillow, closing my eyes. I breathe in and out slowly, not sleeping, just relaxing. It's surprising how calm and serene, and I dare say, sated, one feels after doing something like that.

I'm not sure how much time passes by, but at some point, I hear the shower turn off. I open my eyes slightly, them landing on Avery who enters the room with merely a towel wrapped around his waist. I noticed before, when I first saw him bare-chested, that he has tattoos. Not a lot on his chest, but his arms are covered in them, and when he turns his back to me, I see another one, a big bird taking flight. I wonder what all these tattoos mean, if they even mean anything at all.

He drops the towel and I know I should look away now, or at least close my eyes, but I don't. I can't. I just stare at his behind, his plump bottom. Then he pulls on a pair of underwear, covering himself from me.

He closes the door to his closet and approaches the bed. I immediately close my eyes shut, feeling the dip in the bed when he lies down. I scoot away from him a little, because he's showered now and is clean now while I am not, so he probably doesn't want to touch me right now.

But, boy, am I wrong, because the moment I do, I'm tugged forward into a hard chest. My eyes snap open and meet his.

"What are you doing?" he asks, blinking through his long eyelashes.

"I figured you wouldn't want to touch me right now, because I'm...you know...dirty," I mumble, staring at his chest instead of at his face.

"Why in the world would I not want to touch you?" he exclaims, like he cannot believe his ears. "I can't stop touching you."

My eyes widen, meeting his.

"I never want to stop touching you," he confesses.

A warm feeling spreads throughout my chest.

"I want to take a bath," I suddenly announce. "Will you wash me?"

A smile tugs at his lips, and he nods. He gets out of bed, saying he's going to start running the bath and I nod, laying in his bed with the biggest smile on my face. He never wants to stop touching me. Does that mean...he can possibly...like me?

I really hope so, because I really don't want this to be a one-night stand or a one-time thing. I know I definitely want to see him again after tonight. Maybe start with a date next time.

My cheeks warm up at the thought.

Then I hear him calling me. I excitedly jump out of bed, not even shy that I'm only in a bra and join him in the bathroom. The bathroom is huge, with a toilet, a shower, and a bath. I've never seen a bathroom with both a shower and bath before.

Avery notices my eyes and shrugs, "Sometimes I get lazy."

It's only now that I notice the setup he's made. There are scented candles on the windowsill of a window that has a view of the city and the bath is bubbly itself. He did all of this...for me?

I'm overwhelmed by emotion. Yep. I definitely want to see him again. Maybe even forever.

He holds a hand out to me and I fall into his arms, letting him lift me up and place me in the bath. The water comes up all the way to my collarbone, making me comfortable enough to remove my bra.

He then starts washing me, starting off with my hair, lathering the shampoo into my hair and massaging my scalp with such expert fingers. Then he starts on my body, his hands touching every inch of me.

"Have you done this before?" I ask, leaning my head back against the bath.

"Only for one other person," he answers. I wait for him to continue. "My mom."

It pleases me that it wasn't some other woman he's been with before, but actually his mom. Me being the only one besides his mom getting this treatment from him makes me feel special. I just hope I'm not being too naïve.

When he's done washing me, he helps me out of the tub and wraps me in a fluffy white towel. Then he suddenly picks me up bridal style and I squeal.

"I can walk, you know," I tell him.

"And I told you that I love touching you," he says as a matter of fact. I blush, hiding my face in his shoulder. He carries me back into the bedroom, setting me down on the bed and disappearing into his closet. He comes out with another shirt, a grey one this time. He helps me into it, pulling the towel down from under the shirt.

I love the way he's treating me. Even though I can do all of this on my own, he's still helping me, taking care of me, especially after he put his mouth on me.

We climb back into bed together, his one arm resting under my neck and the other splayed over my stomach. I turn my head to him. There's something I want to ask him, but I'm afraid if I do, it'll change things. Maybe make things awkward, or bad.

"You okay?" he asks, his eyebrows furrowing.

"I'm okay. I'm better than okay. I'm perfect," I say instead of voicing my concerns. He smiles, cuddling closer to me.

"I'm glad. I am too."

I close my eyes, pushing all my concerns away and revelling in how good his touch feels.

This is perfect.

I hope it lasts.

CHAPTER 5 – TAKARA

I wake up in an empty bed.

Stretching out my arms, I sigh in satisfaction. The room is dark, with the curtains still drawn. I sit up.

Where's Avery?

The thought that he may have just left after the night we shared crosses my mind, but only for a brief moment before I remember that this is his own apartment so there's nowhere he could have disappeared to.

I get up from the bed, acutely aware that I'm only wearing Avery's shirt with absolutely nothing underneath. My panties are ripped, lying deserted on the ground, and I have no idea where my bra is. I'll have to ask him, and to do that, I have to try my best not to be embarrassed. This man, Avery...has seen me bare. Yes, I hid my breasts from him, but after seeing everything else, I might as well have just left them hanging open on show for him.

I walk out of the bedroom and down the hallway. I peek around the corner, an immediate smile tugging at my lips when I see him.

Avery. Standing by the stove. In just grey sweatpants that hang low on his hips. Revealing the Calvin Klein band of his underwear. And his back is bare.

I can't help but admire his bare back. The way the muscles contract with every move he makes. I touched those muscles last night. I gripped them so hard when all I could see was stars.

Then he turns around, his eyes landing on me.

A smile flutters onto his face, and he immediately opens his arms, holding them out to me. Unable to stop myself, I rush towards him, throwing myself into his awaiting arms. He embraces me tightly, almost like he missed me.

This feels oddly...intimate. Others might laugh at me for calling this intimate after what we did last night, but this is different. A different

26

kind of intimate. Last night, we were both just consumed by lust for one another and acted on it. But now, him hugging me like this, his touch so gentle, feels different.

A good kind of different. I like it. It makes me feel like there's something more here. More than lust. Maybe something special.

Naïve, huh?

I wish it wasn't.

"How did you sleep?" he asks and I pull away slightly, still in his arms, so that I can look up at him.

"Great," I answer. "You?"

"Best sleep I've had in years."

A frown mars my face.

"Years? Are you okay? Do you suffer from insomnia?" I question, concern in my voice.

"I wouldn't go as far as to say I suffer from insomnia, but something similar to that," is all he says, before pulling away from me. "I hope you're hungry. I made breakfast."

I don't fail in noticing the way he dodges talking about that topic any further, but I don't bring it up again. We don't really know each other, and so he has no obligation to explain things personal to him to me.

"Starving," I say instead, rubbing my stomach.

"Sit. I'll dish you," he says and when he proceeds to dish me breakfast, I sit down on a bar stool at the kitchen island. He joins me soon after, with two plates in his hands. My mouth waters at the sight of what he has made.

Scrambled eggs, sausages, fried tomato and a piece of toast.

"It's not much," Avery says, scratching the back of his neck, and I realize. He's shy.

"It's perfect," I say, unable to stop myself from reaching out and placing my hand on top of his. His eyes widen a fraction, glued to our hands.

Then suddenly, he's reaching for me, and his lips meet mine in a ferocious kiss of passion. I gasp into his mouth, grabbing onto his shoulders. The kiss is over just as quickly as it started, a moan of protest escaping me when he rips himself away from me.

Avery's breathing hard and so am I, still shocked by the sudden kiss.

"Let me take you out," he requests against my lips.

"Like a...date?" I uncertainly ask, my voice small.

"Not like a date," he disagrees. "A date."

I smile, the widest smile I can.

"I'd love that."

*****

Tonight is the date.

I'm hyperventilating.

"I don't think I can do this," I tell Zoe, pacing up and down my bedroom.

"Stop pacing," she scolds, and I come to a reluctant stop. "Look at me. You *can* do this. It's not like this is your first date."

She's right. I went on plenty of dates with Chris throughout our five-month relationship. But this is different, because unlike with Chris, I actually *like* Avery.

"Consider your past dates with Chris as practice for tonight," Zoe says. "Look, I know why you're nervous. This is your first date with someone you actually like."

Zoe knows me so well.

"But there's no need to be. Judging by what you've already told me about this guy and what happened between the two of you, I can say with almost full certainty he likes you too. Which means that you have nothing to worry about. Okay? Any other guy would've been pissed you didn't sleep with them, but him? I think it made him like you even more. Enough to actually make a move and ask you out. I don't see any way tonight can possibly go wrong."

I nod, taking a deep breath.

"Good. In and out. In and out." Zoe guides.

After a few more tries, I'm calm enough to actually get dressed. I had Zoe come over because I needed her fashion advice urgently. Besides, I wasn't sure what the dress code for tonight is. Casual? Formal? Sexy?

Only Zoe can give me a mix of those categories with success.

"So, did he tell you where he's taking you?" Zoe asks, sitting back down on my bed.

"No. Just told me to be ready by 7pm," I say, slipping into the dress. I move to grab a pair of pumps, but Zoe sends me a stern look, handing me a pair of strappy heels instead.

"He's tall. You're gonna need it," is all she says. I don't bother protesting, slipping into the heels before going to stand in front of the human-sized mirror.

Here I stand, dressed in a red dress that hugs all my curves perfectly, stopping just above my knees. I feel more comfortable tonight than I did that night at the club, in that skimpy dress that barely covered my bottom. My hair is styled in its natural waves with a few strands pinned to the back. I wear a simple silver necklace with a silver pendant on it along with a matching bracelet and earrings. The set belongs to my mom and luckily, she's out tonight so I won't be caught wearing them. She hates it when I wear her jewellery. Or anything that belongs to her. I used to love dressing up in her clothes when I was younger, not caring that it was too big for me, but when I grew older and started paying attention to how I appeared, I stopped, especially since my body became very different from hers.

"You look beautiful," Zoe gushes. "Avery is going to lose his mind."

"More than that night in the club?"

"Definitely," she says with absolute certainty.

Then the doorbell rings.

My heart stops.

It's him. *He's* here.

"What are you waiting for? Go open the door." Zoe rushes me, pushing me towards the door.

Taking a deep breath, I open the door.

My breath hitches. There he stands, dressed in a black suit, holding a singular red rose in his hand. My heart melts. I so prefer a single rose over an entire bouquet. Now, I can cherish just the one.

"You look...wow," he breathes out, unblinking. And then he snaps out of it, handing me the rose. "This is for you."

"Thank you," I murmur, feeling shy. Then suddenly, I hear him curse under his breath. I frown. "Everything okay?"

He plasters a smile onto his face. "Everything's fine. Shall we go?"

"Let me just put this in water and grab my purse," I say, walking back into my apartment. I find a thin vase and place the rose in it with a little water. I just grab my purse and am about to walk back to the door when I'm grabbed and pulled around the corner.

"What?" I ask Zoe who stares at me with bright eyes.

"Do you seriously not know?" she questions, staring at me with exasperation. I shake my head.

"Did I do something wrong? Is that why he cursed?" I ask.

"No, if anything, you were too good," she says. I send her a confused look. "You just had to look down, my friend."

Down where? To the floor?

Zoe shakes her head at me.

"He's *hard*, Kara."

Hard? I blink. Once. Twice.

"He got hard just by looking at you," she continues. "Girl, you lucky duck."

I blink once more, but there is no time for her words to sink in before she's pushing me back into Avery's view, and I plaster a quick smile on my face, acting like nothing has happened. I can't help but take a quick glance down at his crotch, my eyes widening slightly when I see the bulge in his pants. If I didn't touch it before, I would have been so shocked by the size. It was a first for me, but even I knew that his package was impressive. I think I even told him that at one point.

"Let's go," he says, grabbing my hand and leading me to his car in the complex parking lot. Like a complete gentleman, he opens the door for me as well as closes it after I'm in the car.

"Where are we going?" I ask him when he's in the car too.

"A little restaurant in town. I figured you might want to go somewhere more private and with less people," he says. "I hope I'm not overstepping?"

"Not at all. I quite appreciate it," I tell him, and it's true. I hate going to crowded places, and that's why I hate going to carnivals, amusement parks, and even taking public transport. Call me spoiled, but I'd rather call a private cab before even considering taking the bus.

He reaches over the console, grabbing my hand. He holds our hands on my upper thigh, a simple gesture, but it's enough to have his skin burning through the fabric of my dress. He drives with one hand, something I've never seen in real life before, but realize I quite appreciate. It's hot, dare I say, or maybe that's because it's him. I don't know if I'd feel the same way about someone else.

"You look very handsome tonight," I tell him, earning a smile from him. I look at his hair, his hair that he didn't bother in taming or styling even for tonight. I'm glad, because I love the way it looks when it's messy. I still need to run my fingers through those thick tresses. It's something I've been itching to do since we met.

We arrive at the restaurant, a small Italian restaurant downtown, but still in the fancy part of town. He once again gets the door for me, placing his hand on the small of my back and leading me inside.

"Table for Avery Wilde," he tells the hostess who immediately leads us to our table.

Wilde. That's his last name.

Avery Wilde.

He just got ten times hotter.

Just like the night we met, we end up at one of the booths in the corner, the fabric a beautiful red velvet colour. Also, just like the night we met, he sits next to me instead of opposite me.

"What would you like to drink?" the hostess, asking Avery more than me.

"Just a bottle of chardonnay with two glasses, please," he orders. Then he adds, "And a jug of water, please, with a slice of lemon."

She nods and walks away. Others might not appreciate him ordering for me, calling him controlling, but I like how he takes charge, not only in the bedroom. I'm quiet and shy, especially around people I don't know, so I appreciate him taking the initiative. It helps that he seems to have a good grasp on what I like.

"What are you feeling like tonight?" he asks.

"Lasagne," I immediately answer. He chuckles and my face warms up in embarrassment.

The hostess brings our drinks and Avery tells her our order, mine being mince lasagne and his being a mushroom pesto pasta.

Then he turns to me. "So, how are you feeling?"

"About?" I ask, sending him a confused look.

"Anything. Everything. Us," he answers. "Like, do you regret coming on this date with me?"

"Not so far." I answer, my tone teasing. I don't think I could ever regret going on a date with this man.

"That's good to hear," he says, his voice laced with relief. "I haven't been on a date in a while and was worried I might have lost my touch."

"Well, we still have all night for you to screw things up," I say and he chuckles.

"I'll try my best," he says, and we both laugh.

I pour myself some water into a glass and wine for him, taking a sip.

"And you? How long has it been since you've been on a date?" he asks, taking a sip of his wine.

"Honestly? The night we met," I admit, and something flashes in his eyes. I feel the need to explain. "My ex and I were on a date when I broke things off with him. Then I went to the bar with a few friends."

"To drink it off?" he asks, the bitterness in his tone catching me off guard.

"No. To celebrate," I tell him honestly. "I didn't really like him, to be honest."

This piques his interest.

"Then why date him?"

I shrug. I don't want to go into the details of why I dated Chris.

"You know, some might consider you going out with me so soon after your breakup a red flag," he says. Panic creeps in.

"Do you?" I ask, slightly fearful of the answer.

"Am I your rebound?" he asks.

"No," I answer immediately. And it's true. In order for him to be my rebound, I would have had to like Chris. Which I didn't. "You'd never be a rebound."

To me. To anyone with eyes.

Then he smiles, his eyes softening before he grabs my hand.

"I don't consider you a red flag," he finally answers my question. "I think you genuinely like me."

I do. God knows I do.

Then his hands are on me, his fingers sliding down my waist and over my hips.

"I know I like you," he says. I smile. Then finally, I reach up, threading my fingers through his hair. It's softer than I imagined. Thicker, too.

"I like you too."

And then I place my lips on his.

Are we going too fast? Did I develop feelings for this man too fast?

Maybe. But I don't care. In these past few days, he's made me feel more than I've ever felt before, and I'm not about to ruin things because I'm scared. If anything, that's fuelling my need to make this work.

"I love kissing you," he breathes out. "I love touching you."

I giggle when he says that, his fingers on my hips.

"I hate this dress," he grumbles. "It's too long."

I giggle again, not at all turned off by what he just said. If anything, this tells me just how much he wants me.

"No," he suddenly says, pulling back. "I like this dress. I change my mind."

"Why?" I ask him, genuinely curious.

"Because no other man should see you in anything skimpy but me." he answers.

I stay quiet, unsure of what to say.

"I hate your ex for seeing you like that," he says, his face turned up into a frown. See me like what? In a skimpy dress, or naked? Because he's the only man who has ever seen me naked, or remotely close to that. But I don't tell him that.

"You jealous?" I tease.

"Yes," he answers easily, surprising me. "If it were possible, I'd make him unsee that."

I giggle.

"Oh? You find this funny?"

I force myself to stop giggling, pursing my lips to keep in my smile.

Then our food comes, and this distracts him. My mouth waters at the sight of lasagne. There's so much cheese. I love it.

I immediately dig in, moaning in satisfaction when I take the first bite. This is by far the best lasagne I've ever had.

I'm busy eating when I notice Avery staring at me in my peripheral.

"What?" I ask with a mouth full of food. Unattractive, I know.

"Nothing," he says. "I just like watching you eat. It's sexy."

I furrow my eyebrows at his words.

"Are you okay?"

"What do you mean?" he asks, him looking confused now.

"You find me devouring my food sexy?" I question. He nods.

When he sees the way I'm looking at him, he says, "Don't judge me. I hate girls who eat little. I prefer my woman to eat and appreciate the food in front of her without caring about who is watching. Including me."

"You do realize they do that so they stay thin right?"

He nods, his hands suddenly grabbing onto my hips.

"That's why I'm glad you don't do that. I love your curves."

My gaze softens.

I look down at his hands on me. I've never really liked my curves, especially since I've always been compared to how my mother looked when she was my age, but now, I feel different. I like the way his hands fit on me. My hips that fit so perfectly in his big hands.

I like it all now.

CHAPTER 6 – TAKARA

I don't want to say goodbye to him.

Not yet.

And that's why we sit in his car that's parked in my complex parking lot. We've been sitting here for the past half hour, neither of us making a move to say bye. He clearly doesn't want to say goodbye to me either.

So somehow, I ended up on his lap in the driver's seat with my lips on his and his fingers in my hair. I swear, there's nothing better than kissing this man, than touching him. He brings out a side in me I had no idea someone like me could ever possess, but I don't hate it. I like it.

Only *he* brings it out in me, though. Only him.

I moan when his free hand that isn't in my hair moves down in between us and starts caressing me through my underwear.

"Fuck," he curses, breaking away from me. "I need *some* part of me to be inside you. Please say yes. Please, baby."

"Yes," I whisper, and he wastes no time in grabbing onto the thin fabric of my panties and sheds it completely, causing me to gasp. I'm still yet to get used to that.

Then he dips a single finger inside me, and I wince at the slight burn from the intrusion. This is very different from having his tongue inside me. It's bigger, too. To my dismay, Avery notices my reaction and pulls free.

"Kara..."

"I'm okay," I assure him, resting my hands on his shoulders. "Don't stop. Please."

There's a small frown that lingers on his face, but he listens to me and slides his finger back inside me, slower this time, giving me more time to adjust to the intrusion. He kisses me, though, distracting me from the slight burn.

I kiss him back, moving my lips against his as he starts to move his finger inside me. In and out. In and out.

"More," I whimper.

He listens, adding another finger, stretching me so deliciously, I don't feel any pain anymore.

"That...that feels good, Avery."

"Yes," he encourages. "Say my name, baby."

Without thinking, I unbuckle his pants and take his cock out of his underwear, stroking my hand up and down his shaft. He throws his head back but doesn't stop moving his fingers inside me.

We move together, chasing each other's high, and soon, we both slip off the edge and come, his release splashing onto my hand while mine drenches his fingers in it.

He pulls his fingers out of me and brings them to his mouth before licking my release off them. God, that has to be the hottest thing I've ever seen.

Then he kisses me, so that I can taste myself on his tongue. This is so addictive. If I could, I'd never stop –

Knock knock.

We both jump in surprise, our lips parting.

I freeze in his arms and I turn my head to the side, bracing myself to see some random stranger standing outside the car. But nothing could have braced myself for who I see.

My mother.

CHAPTER 7 – AVERY

All the colour drains from Kara's face.

I look at the window, surprise flashing in my eyes when I see a familiar face.

"Baby, that's –"

Kara cuts me off by jumping off my lap and onto the passenger seat, starting to pull her dress back onto her body. I understand her reaction. We almost got caught. Or maybe we will still get caught. But other than what we were doing in the car just now, there's no reason to be embarrassed. We're both adults, *consenting* adults, so it should be okay.

I follow Kara, tucking myself back into my pants and buckling up. I reach out to Kara, making her freeze.

"Let me help you," I say and she nods, albeit reluctantly, which I don't understand. Why is she suddenly hesitant about letting me touch her all of a sudden?

I grab tissues from the car's cubbyhole and start wiping myself off her before helping her into her dress and when I'm certain we're both presentable, I roll my tinted window down.

"Mrs. Smith. What brings you here?" I say, pleasantly. She smiles upon seeing that it's me, although, surprise still flashes in her eyes.

"I should be asking you that, Professor Wilde," she says with a chuckle.

"Please. We're not at work. Call me Avery," I say with a smile.

"Alright then, Avery," she says, her eyes lighting up. "Anyway, what brings you to my complex?"

"You live here?" I ask, surprised. She nods.

"On the top floor, with my daughter," she says.

"Oh, I see," I say with a nod. "I'm here dropping off my –"

I stop talking abruptly when I turn my head to introduce Kara as my date, but she's not there. Where did she go?

I get out of my car, closing the door shut and looking around.

Mrs. Smith looks confused. "You looking for someone?"

"Uh...well –" I stop talking again when I see the sight of a body bent over on the passenger side of my car. I see the red dress, the dress I just helped a certain brunette with hazel eyes put back on.

She's hiding. But why? Is she maybe...embarrassed to be seen with me? No way. I feel insulted.

"I should go," I say, turning back to Mrs. Smith. "It was nice seeing you."

"Wait," she suddenly says, grabbing onto my arm. "You can't just leave like that. Let me at least invite you in for a drink."

"That's really not necessary," I start to say but she waves me off.

"It's the least I can do...Avery," she says my name like she's testing it on her tongue. I think I get it. Up until now, I've just been Professor Wilde to her since we've never seen one another outside of work before, and I know she's just trying to be nice by inviting me into her home for a drink, but I'm really not in the mood right now. Not with my *date* still hiding behind my car.

I still can't believe it. I thought she liked me. Maybe she does, but clearly not enough to want to be seen with me.

"I really can't –"

"Kara?" Mrs. Smith cuts in, her eyebrows furrowing.

Then Kara slowly and hesitantly rises up from her hiding spot, her eyes fearful, like she got caught doing something she shouldn't have. She avoids my eyes, her gaze glued on Mrs. Smith.

"What are you doing? What were you doing? Why were you hiding behind Avery's car?" Mrs. Smith questions, but I'm confused. Do they know each other. Maybe they're neighbours.

"Mom," Kara says and my eyes widen. Did she just call Mrs. Smith mom?

"Why are you dressed like that? Where have you just come from?" Mrs. Smith continues with her questions despite not getting a single answer.

Kara doesn't say anything.

"Where were you?"

"I was on a date," Kara suddenly bursts out.

"A date?" Mrs. Smith – her mother – repeats, and Kara nods. Is she going to tell her mom she was on a date with me? Finally? "Oh, okay."

Mrs. Smith sounds distracted, and then her eyes land on me again and they light up.

"Avery, this is Kara, my daughter," she introduces. "Kara, this is Mr. Wilde. He's a professor at the university."

Kara's eyes widen. I watch as they fill with realization, and then horror.

Why horror? Does she not like that I teach for a living? I didn't peg her to be judgemental.

"Avery," Mrs. Smith calls out, grabbing my attention. "Kara will be a freshman at the university in a few weeks."

Everything stops.

"I'm sorry – what?" I blurt out, unsure if I heard her correctly.

"She's a new student at the university."

My eyes nearly bulge out of their sockets.

Now I understand the horror.

"And she will be studying history, your subject."

So, not only is she a student at the university I work at, but she's also going to be *my* student?

Fuck me.

CHAPTER 8 – TAKARA

There's an awkward silence.

I can't believe it. The man I just went out on a date with, the man who took my first kiss, the man who *touched* me, is my soon-to-be professor.

Avery looks just as horrified as I do. He too had no idea.

Good. I don't know what I would have done if I had to find out he knew. But not so good. He's going to be my professor.

I don't know what to say. Especially in front of my mother. Do I smile and pretend I don't know him? Or do I confess that we were just on a date? No way. I can't do that.

"Let's go up," Mother suddenly says. Wait, what? Oh right. She invited him up for a drink.

He still hasn't said yes. Please say no. Please just be on your way. I'm begging you, Avery.

"Sure," he says instead and starts following my mother out of the parking lot. What the hell? Did he just say yes? Why in the world would he say yes?

"Kara," my mother calls out. "You coming?"

"I'm coming," I call out after her, following behind them.

By the time we get to the top floor and by the door of our apartment, Avery pulls me to the side slightly, his hand on the small of my back, discretely murmuring, "We need to talk."

This is what I was dreading. This is why I wanted him to leave. I don't want to talk to him. I know we need to, but I don't want to. Right now, I just want to crawl into bed and sleep, hoping to sleep this all away. Not have a drink with him and my mother.

Instead of saying any of that though, I just nod, immediately leaving his touch to walk inside. Luckily, Zoe left hours ago, using her spare key to lock.

"What do you like to drink, Avery? We have quite the few options here," my mother says. My mother is quite the liquor lover. She spends most of her nights locked up in her bedroom with a bottle of wine. There's not a time I remember where she didn't have a glass of alcohol in her hands. I wouldn't say she has a problem and when she gets drunk, she doesn't bother me. She just sleeps it off. Although, I doubt she'll allow herself to indulge in an entire bottle tonight, not in front of Avery, her co-worker. Oh right. I should probably start calling him Professor Wilde. But I don't want to. That takes out all the intimacy of our relationship. I don't want that. Just...not yet.

"I like whiskey," Cameron answers and I recall the night we met at the bar. That night, he was drinking a glass of whiskey too. I don't know why I remember that. Heck, I remember everything about him.

"Alrighty then. Let me just go get us glasses," my mother says, but just before she can walk to the kitchen, Cameron stops her.

"Can I use your bathroom, please?" he asks.

"Of course," my mother answers easily. "Kara, be a dear and show Avery where the bathroom is."

Be a dear? She's never spoken to me this nicely before. Of course, this is an act she's putting on for Avery, who she seems quite fond of, which is a shocker, because I didn't know she could be fond of anything.

Ignoring the anxiety tumbling through my stomach in waves, I lead Avery to the bathroom. Our apartment is not as glamorous or nearly as big as his, but he doesn't judge.

"This is it," I say and I'm about to walk away when he suddenly grabs my arm and pulls me inside with him. He shuts the door, clicking the lock before pushing me against the door, trapping me in with his body. "What are you doing?!"

"I told you we need to talk," he feels the need to remind me.

"Here?" I exclaim with big eyes. Then I shake my head. "No. It's dangerous. My mom could come looking for me at any minute and if she finds me in here with you...no."

"It won't take long," he promises.

My eyes stay glued to the ground. I can't bare to look at him right now. If I do, I might break down. And trust me, no one wants to see that. I tend to cry big fat ugly tears. Very unattractive.

"Please look at me," he softly requests, but I shake my head. Then he adds, "Please, baby."

My head snaps up to his at the pet name. He's still calling me that, even after what's been revealed tonight?

When he reaches out to touch me, I swat his hand away.

"We can't," I say. "This is wrong."

I'm looking down once more.

"I know," he breathes out. "But I told you this before. I can't stop touching you."

"Well, you have to. Especially in front of my mom," I tell him. If she catches onto anything, we're both screwed. I'm surprised she didn't catch onto anything back in the parking lot, with me hiding behind his car. She still hasn't asked what he was doing here in the first place since the first time.

"Is it over now? Between us?" he asks and my head snaps up to his, my eyes accusatory.

"Are you seriously asking me this right now?" I snap. "I just found out who you really are. This is not just new to you. It's new to me too. I never imagined the first man I would actually like would turn out to be my professor."

By the time I'm done talking, well, basically yelling at him, I'm out of breath.

Then he's pulling me into his arms and he embraces me tightly.

"You think I expected this? This is the last thing I expected to happen," he says into my hair, his grip on me tightening when I don't hug him back. I can't. My arms are limp, at my sides. "It would just be my luck. I find someone I'm truly interested after being single for years, and she happens to be my student."

"Thanks for close captioning our situation," I mumble, quite bitterly. He chuckles, but even that sounds quite bitter.

He pulls away but still keeps his hands on me, as if he can't help but touch me. I know he can't.

"What do we do now?" I ask him.

"I don't know," he says. "I *really* don't know."

"Didn't you ask me if things are over between us because that's what you want?" I ask and his eyes become hard at my words.

"You really think that's what I want?!" he bursts out. Now he's angry, and it shows. "I don't want any of this. I don't want you to be my student. I don't want to be your professor."

"Then what do you want?"

"You!" he exclaims. "I've wanted you since I first laid my eyes on you."

I don't know what to say. The fact that this man, yes, *man*, still wants me even after finding out that I'm his student speaks volumes. It might be considered a red flag to others, but to me, I couldn't care less. Because I feel the same way.

Unable to stop myself, I reach up, wrapping my arms around his neck, and kiss him. It's a soft kiss, one where we pour all our feelings and desires for one another into. Avery pulls me flush against him, but there's nothing sexual about the way we touch. No, all we want to do right now is kiss. Nothing more. There's not even any tongue involved. This is the first closed mouth kiss we've shared, but even this, I love. Because everything with him is perfect.

I pull away first, knowing that just as innocent that kiss was, within seconds, it can turn into something more, something more that we should probably avoid for now.

He cups my face in his hands, caressing my skin gently.

"You're so perfect," he murmurs. I shake my head.

"I'm not," I disagree.

"You are," he insists. "No matter who I am or who you are or how big our age gap is, you're perfect for me. I believe that."

I can tell from his eyes; he really does believe that. I wish I could be as confident as him. I am confident in my feelings for him, but where we go from now? I have no idea.

"How old are you, by the way?" I ask him, something I've been wondering since we met. I knew when I first saw him that he's older than me, but it can't be by that much, right? I mean, he still looks so young.

"Thirty," he answers. That is older than I thought.

"Birthday?"

"September 12th," he answers again. So, he's going to be thirty-one this year. And I just turned nineteen. That makes him...12 years older than me. Oh, wow. "I can practically see the gears running in your head right now. Why? Am I too old for you?"

"You're twelve years older than me," I find myself telling him.

"Oh," is all he says. There are a few long moments of silence before he finally speaks again. "Does it bother you that much?"

Not as much as I thought it would. I'm just...surprised. Yeah, let's go with that.

I shake my head at his question.

"It's not that. It's just...I'll admit. It is bigger than I expected. I thought you'd be twenty-five at most," I say.

"What kind of professor is twenty-five years old?" he can't help but sound incredulous in his question.

"Yeah. I know. I'm stupid," I mutter.

"I never said that," he defends. Then when I don't respond, he murmurs, "Baby."

"You call me that one more time and I'll really lose it," I warn.

"And what will you do? Kiss me again?" he retorts, amusement in his voice.

"Don't tease me," I snap, trying my best to glare at him. "You don't know this about me yet, but I'm batshit crazy."

A smile flirts with his lips. His eyes sparkle.

"You know that's the first time I've heard you use a swear word," he says.

"So what? What are you going to do?" I question, thrusting my chest out to seem intimidating. But it doesn't work. It only draws his attention to my breasts, his pupils dilating.

Then he leans forward, his mouth by my ear.

"Have you ever heard me swear before?" he murmurs, his warm breath on my ear. I gulp, shaking my head. I know he's done it, but none of which I've heard clearly. Then he pushes himself against me, forcing my back against the wall. "Fuck."

My eyes flutter closed, a breath leaving me.

"I want to fuck you so badly, baby."

My breath hitches. I shouldn't be this turned on. I really shouldn't. But...

Then suddenly, there's a knock on the door. Mom.

"You still alright in there?" I hear my mother ask.

"Yes. I'll be out soon," Avery responds and then I hear retreating footsteps.

I release a breath I didn't even know I was holding. We almost got caught, again.

"I have to go," I say, reaching for the lock.

"We're not done here," C warns.

Oh, I know we're not. We're far from done.

CHAPTER 9 – AVERY

Kara is drunk.

So is her mother.

"Avery," Mrs. Smith calls out, holding a glass of wine in between her fingers, but barely. It looks ready to tip over any second. "Do you know how hot you are?"

I instantly feel uncomfortable. Is Kara's mother perhaps...hitting on me?

No. There's no way. Mrs. Smith should be forty at the oldest considering the way she looks, and admittedly, she's closer to my age than Kara is, but I'm not looking to go there. Despite the age difference, I want her daughter, not her.

"Mom," Kara suddenly jolts up from her two-minute nap, seeming more awake than ever. "I don't think he knows."

"Kara, how can he not know?" Mrs. Smith whispers to Kara, like they're sharing a secret. "I mean, look at him. If it weren't completely unprofessional, I would be on him like bees on honey."

I don't think that's the smartest analogy, but Kara seems to get it because she nods.

"No!" Kara yells out, startling me slightly. "You can't have him." Then she looks at me, and smiles. "He's mine."

In that moment, butterflies flutter in the depths of my belly. God, it's been so long since I've felt that, I thought that maybe the part of me that feels emotions like this was dead.

Then she crawls across the couch and onto my lap. I panic slightly, but then I see that her mother has passed out on the floor, the glass lying tipped over by her head with wine spilling out onto the carpet. Luckily it's white wine and not red, cause that shit stains.

"You're mine, right?" Kara says more than asks.

I can't stop the smile that tugs at my lips, my hands automatically landing on her hips. It's become a habit of mine, to touch her there whenever she's within arm's reach.

"Answer!" she suddenly exclaims. I nod.

"I'm yours," I agree and she smiles quite triumphantly.

"Yay!" she cheers, before collapsing onto me. Soft snores escape her mouth and I chuckle. I smooth the hair out of her face, smiling when she drools a little. She's so cute.

Man, I've got it bad for this girl, and I'm done trying to convince myself otherwise. If anything, what happened tonight was an eye-opener for me. The realization that I might lose her made me realize just how much she means to me. We don't know each other that long, but somehow, she has burrowed her way into my cold heart and made me feel again.

It's a miracle.

I don't know how long I just sit there, with her sleeping in my arms before I decide it's time that I should put her to bed. I stand up with her in my arm, glancing at her mother.

It would be inappropriate of me to take her to bed, right? Yep, definitely.

I'm not sure which room is Kara's, but the moment I reach a certain door, I *know* it's her room. Her room doesn't scream overly girly and there's no posters of boy bands plastered everywhere, so that's a good thing. Her room basically just consists of a bed, a desk, and a comfy looking poof. Now that is pink. It's cute.

I carry her to her bed, using my one hand to pull back the covers before placing her in the bed and covering her. I sit down next to her sleeping form, once again moving her hair out of her face.

Then her eyes flutter open.

"Are we over?" she suddenly asks.

"No," I shake my head. "We're far from over."

A smile graces her lips and she nods, before her eyes close and she returns to dreamland. I'm halfway convinced to stay here with her all night, but her mother catching us in the morning convinces me otherwise.

So, I get up and make my way out of the apartment. I feel slightly bad for leaving her mother on the floor like that so I just placed a pillow under her head, although, her body is going to hurt in the morning. Nothing I can do about that. I refuse to touch her like that. Especially after she called me hot.

I'm in my car when my phone rings. The name, Gloria, flashes on the screen, and I frown. Why is my ex of three years calling me? We haven't spoken since the breakup, so why? Then another name appears on top. Chloe.

I smile, pressing answer on the screen on my dashboard.

"*How you doing, baby brother?*" Chloe's voice filters in through the call. I roll my eyes. She's only two years older than me, but she treats me like I'm a complete decade younger than her.

"I'm good. You?"

"*Great. Zach is finally sleeping through the night so that's a good thing,*" Zach is my nephew and Chloe's newborn baby. Well, I guess he's about four months now, so not really newborn anymore. "*Anything new going on with you?*"

I immediately think about Kara. Chloe is the one person I trust to tell everything to, because I know that she won't just blab everything to our parents. Not even her husband, although, he's cool.

"*Ooh, I know that silence,*" she suddenly says. "*You met someone, didn't you?*"

Her knowing me so well has proven to be both a blessing and a curse multiple times.

"*So?*" she prompts. "*Who is she? What's her name? How did you two meet? I want all the details!*"

She sounds more excited than me about this, and that's saying something.

"Her name is Takara. We met at a bar."

"*Oh? One nightstand?*" she asks.

"Not your conventional one nightstand. We didn't sleep together, just fooled around a little," I admit.

"*And you wanted more?*"

"Yes," I admit.

"*Surprising,*" she says, and I know why. While I haven't picked up *that* many girls at bars and clubs, I've never wanted to be more with them. It was just sex. That was it. We'd have fun in the sheets at some hotel without even exchanging names and then go our separate ways once we're both satisfied. That was one of my rules. Never tell the girl my name, or at least not my real name, but I broke that the moment Kara asked me for my name. "*She must be special then.*"

"She is," I confess. "At least to me."

"*Wow, I can't believe it. My baby brother is finally growing up,*" she coos.

"I grew up a long time ago, Chloe. In case you've forgotten, I've been in relationships before. I've liked girls before," I remind her.

"*Yeah, but you've never loved anyone before,*" she reminds me.

Yeah. That's the main reason why none of my previous romantic relationships have lasted. I have no problem committing to a girl, but I don't love. It's not like I choose not to. It's just that I *can't*. I just don't think that's wired into my DNA. And that's always been a problem. Because girls would fall in love with me and then at some point, expect a marriage proposal, something I couldn't give them. Then I'd break things off.

"Speaking of never having loved a girl before, Gloria just called me," I tell her.

"*Oh, lord. What does that bitch want all of a sudden?*" Chloe curses.

Gloria was my most recent girlfriend, a girl who dumped me three years ago because once again, I couldn't put a ring on her finger. In her defence, she'd have accepted even a promise ring, but I just couldn't give that to her. Not even that. And that pissed her off.

Chloe, however, never liked Gloria. I'm not sure why, because Gloria was a decent person. While she wasn't always the nicest, she was never outright rude and remained faithful to me throughout our two-year relationship. So, I never had any problems with her. Chloe just justified her hate towards Gloria as a gut feeling that told her Gloria was bad news. So imagine how happy Chloe was when she heard we ended things. Over the moon.

"I don't know. I didn't answer." I shrug.

"*And you don't need to. You have no obligations towards her anymore,*" Chloe reminds me, even though I know that better than anyone else.

Besides, I've got Kara now. Well, I don't *have* her yet, and I'm not sure where we stand with one another right now, but I'm willing to put in the effort to make things work. I just hope she doesn't decide she doesn't want me anymore once she's sober in the morning.

Chloe and I continue talking as I drive home and say our goodbyes once I reach the apartment building. I take a quick shower before climbing into bed, an empty bed.

That night, I dream of Kara.

CHAPTER 10 – TAKARA

I wake up to someone yanking my body up and down.

"What the hell?!" I yell out, pushing the person to the back with such a force, I hear an 'oomph'. I'm in so much pain that I can hardly care right now though. I groan, rolling onto my side and pressing half of my face into the pillow.

"Takara Smith! How dare you throw your best friend to the ground?!" I hear Zoe burst out. I merely groan in response. She's way too loud for this early in the morning. Then she's jumping onto my bed, pulling me onto my back. "Look, I have news."

I pop one eye open to look at her.

"And it's that important that you're waking me up so early?" I ask, my voice groggy.

"It's two in the afternoon, you drunk," she says, shoving me. I groan, turning my head to look at the clock. Two in the afternoon. Indeed, it is. "But before I share my news, care to tell me why both you and your mom are heavily hung over right now? I mean, your mom is always cool and collected and maintains her ladylike composure, but I just saw her throwing up in the kitchen sink."

Her eyes are big like she still cannot believe what she saw.

"And you look like you're not far from that point either," she points out.

I can tell that she's a bit worried I might throw up on her any second now, but I'm all out. I lost count of how many times I got up during the night to puke my guts out, and just when I thought it was over, I felt it coming again. My mother wasn't any better. But she's still vomiting today because she drank a lot more than me. Like I said before, I'm a lightweight.

What even possessed me to drink so much last night? I got completely hammered, and in front of Avery of all people. Groaning, I run my fingers through my wild waves.

"Just tell me your news," I say to Zoe, gesturing for her to talk with a wave of my hand. I'm still waking up and my head still feels like it's about to be split open into two, but she wouldn't be here unless it wasn't important.

"Okay," Zoe starts off, and I can tell that whatever she's about to talk about, she's excited by it. "So, I held off on talking to you about this because you were distracted by your hottie from the bar. But the truth is, I too met someone that night. Just after you left with Avery."

She left with someone? This is slowly waking me up.

"And?" I prompt.

"And a week later, I have a boyfriend," she announces. What? My eyes finally open fully and blink at her. "Look, his name is Derek. He's a little older than us, but he's so sweet. I mean, he didn't even force me to sleep with him that night, and by the way I was kissing him, he knew that that was exactly what I wanted."

"So? Did you sleep with him?" I ask. She shakes her head.

"That's the greatest thing. I went home with him, and we just...talked. It was completely different from what I've experienced before, but I liked it. For the first time, it felt like I didn't have to put out to be interesting to someone," she explains, a genuine smile on her face.

"Well, as long as you're happy, I'm happy," I say, placing my hand on top of hers.

"I am. I really am" she says, her eyes bright from just talking about him. Do I look like that when I talk about Avery?

"But you said he's older. How much older?" I ask, selfishly hoping he's also thirty like Avery so I don't have to feel so ashamed about liking my professor.

"Like twenty-three. He's a senior at the university," Zoe answers. Twenty-three. Nope. Not even near enough to Avery.

"Anyway, enough about me. How was your date? And please explain it thoroughly so I can understand why you got hammered with your mom afterwards," she says, narrowing her eyes slightly.

And that was all it took. I blurt out everything, and when I say everything, I mean *everything*, including how we almost got caught doing...stuff in his car.

Zoe blinks. Once. Twice.

Her silence worries me. Is she judging me right now? I trust that she'd never do that, but then again. I'm the last person she'd ever think to be in this situation.

Then she says the last thing I ever imagined she would say, "You lucky duck."

What?

"And here I thought my romance was gonna be sort of forbidden since he's like four years older than me, but you've got a whole ass man up here sniffing at your goods," Zoe exclaims.

"Shh!" I shush her. My mother may be hungover, but I still can't take any chances.

"So? What happens now?" Zoe asks, her eyes wide with mischief. "Are you two now going to embark on a forbidden romance of some sort?"

"Why does this excite you so much?" I question, now narrowing *my* eyes at her.

"Because this is the closest thing I've gotten to my favourite book. You can't expect me to not be excited by this. Are you not?"

"Excited? Are you insane? I'm mortified," I exclaim. "I can't date my professor. That's unethical and just...straight up wrong."

"Or straight up sexy," Zoe adds.

"Look, I don't know what to do, Zoe," I whine.

"Look, based on what you told me, it seems like he's not going to give up on you two. He wants you enough to ignore the age gap and the fact that he'll be your professor in a few weeks. That says a lot," Zoe says.

"You don't think that's red flag?"

"Girl, are you seriously asking me that?" she asks, sending me an incredulous look. "You know I live for red flags."

"Says the girl who's dating probably the greenest flag ever," I retort. She rolls her eyes at me.

"Look, all I'm saying is, don't break things off just yet. At least find out what it is that he exactly wants from you. Then make your decision. Because from the looks of it, you really like him, and I've known you long enough to confidently tell you this won't happen again anytime soon."

She knows me and my useless feelings too well.

"Now, how about you freshen up, get the stench of vomit out of your mouth, and go see him? I'll drive you."

I don't protest. I do know where he lives, so that should be easy. The only problem is, he might not even be home. Since he teaches at the university, he should be on holiday right now, but who knows. Maybe he has other plans during the day, like exercising and whatnot.

However, I don't let the endless possibilities hinder me from my goal. Today is the day. I'm going to find out exactly what he wants from me and hopefully, make a decision about what I want too.

After I'm done dressing and making sure my mother is safely tucked in her bed, Zoe drives me to Avery's apartment building. Zoe practically drools at the building. I probably mimicked her the first time I was here. She should come here at night, with all the lights on. Then she'd probably shit herself.

"Good luck, my friend. You got this," Zoe says before I get out of the car. She tells me she'll wait for ten minutes in case anything happens before driving away, which I appreciate, because this can go either way.

I take the elevator to the top floor. I'm about to knock on the door when I realize that I's open slightly ajar. I hear voices from the inside of the penthouse, Avery's voice, and another. A woman's voice.

I push the door open slightly more and peak inside. My eyes find Avery first, and he looks just as mouth-watering as ever, even in just a pair of sweatpants and a plain t-shirt. Opposite him stands a woman, tall in her tall heels and her short blonde hair. I'd think she was maybe his sister, but no sister looks at her brother the way this woman is staring at Avery. In fact, as they talk, she's undressing him with her eyes. Something I know I do a lot.

Something twists inside of me. Something ugly.

Who is this woman?

I'm not close enough to make out what they're saying, but the intensity between them and the way she just casually brushes her hand along his bare tattoo-covered arm tells me that they're familiar with one another. Maybe a little *too* familiar for my liking.

I'm stuck on what to do. Do I just keep standing here until they're done? Do I walk in and announce my presence? Do I leave? I'm at a loss. For the first time since meeting him.

With him, everything has always come so naturally, but for the first time, I'm confused, and even...hurt, and I don't even know who this woman is yet.

I take another long look at her and then down at myself. There's a distinct difference between us. I'm a girl, whereas she is a woman. That much is obvious. She's quite put together, even her bob, all gelled back with not a strand out of place. She's his age. Avery's.

Now is the time for me to decide what to do. If I leave now, I might still find Zoe downstairs.

But I don't want to leave. Not without knowing who this woman is first.

So I decide. I'm just going to watch. This whole thing unfold. Whatever this is.

Then Cameron takes a sudden step towards the door, and because of this, I hear him say, "You should go."

"Why?" the woman whines after him, breaking her cool composure. "We're good together. You know that."

"I can't give you what you want," Avery exasperates, turning back to her.

"It's not like I'm asking you to bear your children, Cameron. All I'm asking for is another chance," she says.

"Then what, Gloria? We date for a few years and what? Then you expect marriage from me again. What if I can't give that to you? It'll just be a repeat of when and why we broke up in the first place."

"I've changed, Avery," she says, taking a step closer to him. "I've matured. I realized that I don't need a piece of paper to tie us together. I'm okay with not getting married, as long I know I have you."

Tears fill my eyes. What the hell is going on?

So, I've found out who the woman is. She's his ex, and she wants to get back together with him. And what is this about marriage? He'll never be able to give it to her?

I'm not even sure I understand everything fully, but I feel hurt. Why is he even entertaining this woman and what she's saying? Why...when he has me?

Maybe he still has feelings for her. Feelings that surpass his feelings he has for me by far.

"Avery..." the woman, Gloria, reaches out to him, and then suddenly, I'm pushing the door forward and open completely. Both their heads snap to me, Avery's eyes widening while hers narrow in confusion.

"I-I'm sorry to interrupt. I was just..." What was I doing? Oh, right. I was spying on them.

"Who are you?" *she* is the first to speak.

"I...I'm Kara, and...I'm no one. Really," I mumble, feeling quite helpless in this very moment.

"Baby..."

"Baby?!" Gloria exclaims.

"I should go," I say and start walking away. Cameron follows after me with a 'wait' before grabbing my arm and pulling me to a stop. I turn to him. "You should go back to her."

"What the hell are you talking about?" he questions, sounding truly confused.

"I said you should go to her. Clearly, you two have some history and she wants you back. She clearly loves you, so you should take her back." Why am I even saying this? I don't mean any of this.

"Kara-"

"I'm being serious, Avery," I cut in, lifting my eyes to meet his. "I can't give you what you want. The truth is, I'm just a girl. I can't be the woman you want to be with."

"Where is this all coming from?"

"I came here to make a decision," I say. "And seeing you with her made me realize that this was never going to work. I just deluded myself into thinking that I could make it work, somehow. That if I liked you enough, it wouldn't matter that you're twelve years older than me or that you're my professor. But I was wrong. Maybe if we met when I was older, more mature. But right now, I'm just a little girl. And I'm choosing to say goodbye to you."

He's completely frozen, unblinking.

Standing on my tippy toes, I press a soft kiss to his cheek.

And then I leave. And he doesn't follow me this time.

CHAPTER 11 – AVERY

3 weeks later

The first day back at work.

It finally arrived.

As I make my way to my lecture hall, I try to be okay. Pretend I haven't spent the last three weeks drinking myself in a stupor. I try to pretend last night didn't happen, when I drunkenly climbed into bed with a stranger, imagining it was *her* the entire time.

Takara. Takara Smith. My student as of today.

God, I miss her. I never knew it was possible to miss someone so much, especially when you don't even know them for that long. But I miss her. So much that I lost control, the day before college started. Fuck.

I don't usually swear, both in and outside my head, but I can't help it. I'm fucked up. She fucked me up. I should blame her for the way I feel. I want to...but I can't. Why? Because of the look on her face when she said goodbye to me. She was broken, hurt, and I know it was all my fault.

Shaking Kara off my mind, I walk into the campus History building. My class is on the third floor, and there are only four floors in the building, the first three with lecture halls and the top with the lecturers' offices.

I walk straight to my office on the fourth floor, halting when I see a figure standing right outside my office door. I freeze, recognizing that figure. How could I not? Those long legs clad in a tight skinny jean, those wide hips, the dip of her waist. I remember it all. I touched them all.

Kara.

She looks nervous as she stands there. Does she know it's my office? Of course she does. My name is on the door, in big bold letters that is nearly impossible to miss.

What do I do? I can't just keep standing here like a fool. She's clearly here to see me. Why? I have no idea. But I guess I'll have to find out.

Clearing my throat, I approach her. Upon hearing me, she turns, our eyes meeting. I'm instantly blown away. She looks good. No. She looks *amazing*. Gorgeous. Breathtaking. Sexy. All of the above.

Her features have matured in the last three weeks and her hazel eyes shine brighter than ever. I can't help but wonder if she looks so good because I'm no longer in her life. If so, that's about to change.

"Professor Wilde," she breathes out, breaking the silence. As if she can't help herself, her eyes take me in, quite hungrily might I add, before meeting mine again, her cheeks turning red. She's as affected as I am. Good.

"Ka-Ms. Smith," I greet. "How may I help you?"

Surprise flashes in her eyes. Yes, she probably wasn't expecting this level of professionalism from me. What did she expect me to do though? Jump her the first chance I get? I'm better than that. She should know that.

"Uh...I had a question about the semester syllabus," she stammers, her eyes suddenly unable to meet mine.

"And it couldn't wait until class?" I question, sounding harsher than I meant to. She flinches in response, and I bite my lip to prevent a curse from tumbling out of my mouth. "Let me just unlock my office and we can speak inside."

She wordlessly nods, looking everywhere but at me. I unlock the door with my key and invite her in. She takes in my office while I set my bag onto my desk. I glance at my wristwatch. There's only fifteen minutes until class and I still have to set up the lecture hall, meaning we don't have much time. I can't help but feel disappointed. A part of me wishes I came to work earlier. I mean, how long has she been standing there, waiting for me?

"Your question?" I speak, grabbing her attention. She nods, scrambling to grab a printed page from her backpack and placing it on the desk between us. I notice the first term's textbook sticking from the bag. She's clearly prepared. Good girl.

"Well-there was something...if I can just find it on the page..." She's all over the place, her fingers trembling as she drags it across the page. "I'm sorry. I'm not usually this unorganized. I realize we don't have much time till class starts –"

"Kara," I cut her off, and I can see that she's relieved I stopped her rambling. I can't help but place my hand on her arm. Her skin burns under my touch. "Please calm down."

She stares up at me with hesitant eyes, before slowly nodding. I remove my hand from her arm before I have the urge to touch her some more, and in other places, especially when she appears so nervous in front of me. Clearly, she didn't give it much thought before coming here.

No, I'm wrong. I see it in her eyes. This was *all* she could think about.

"Why don't you take a breather and we can revisit your question after class, if it's still necessary?" I offer her an out and she nods, grateful for it.

Then silence engulfs us. She knows she should go now. I know that class is starting soon and I should go set up. But neither of us make a move.

And then softly, she speaks, so softly, I almost don't hear her, "How are you?"

My eyes snap up in surprise. I know exactly how much it took out of her to ask that question first. I've been contemplating when the time is right to ask her, but she beat me to it.

"I'm okay," I say. "You?"

"Me too," she says. Then more silence.

"You should get going," I break the silence. "Classes are starting soon."

As much as I don't want her to leave just yet, I can't keep her here. She can't be here.

She nods, muttering a soft goodbye before walking out.

Shrugging the feeling of sudden abandonment off, I take my lunch out of my bag, place it on the desk and then I'm headed to the lecture hall. When I get there, Kara is already in her seat, and is taking out her things for class.

I set things up for class and by the time I'm done, it's already past 8.

"Right. Good morning everyone. I am Professor Wilde and I will be your history lecturer this semester," I introduce myself.

A student raises their hand and I nod.

"Only this semester? What about next semester?" she asks.

"If my schedule allows me," I answer.

The number of students here is a lot less than I expected, although, I'm not surprised. Students don't like history as much anymore and only take it if they need to, never mind majoring in it. But Kara is different. She loves history. I can tell, not only from the fact that she's majoring in it.

My eyes unconsciously move to her, and I'm slightly startled when I find her already staring at me. Well, of course she's staring at you. You're the professor. And she's not the only one. Every student is staring at you right now. Stupid.

I shake my head, looking away from her.

"Since we are a small class this semester, how about we go around and introduce ourselves and why we want to study history?" I say and then gesture to the student at the very front to start. The introductions go by in a blur, and then it's *her* turn.

"Um...my name is Kara, and I'm studying history because I find it interesting. There's no real special reason. I just like learning about the past and also comparing it to modern life," she says. I nod, and then we're moving onto the next student.

"So, Professor Wilde," someone calls out. I see that it's the girl from earlier. "Tell us about you. Why did you decide to teach history?"

"Because it's easy," I shrug. "Unlike other subjects, I don't have to make things up or interpret anything. I just have to remember things. And then relay them over to you."

"So, basically, he's dumb," a male student whispers, but loudly enough for me to hear, and a few students snicker.

"Yes, that's right, Mr. I chose to study history because I didn't qualify for anything else," I say before I can stop myself. His eyes widen, both in shock and in panic.

"How do you know that?" he splutters out.

"I know everything, Luke. Not just about you, but about every student in this lecture hall right now. Although, I should warn you. Just because you think history is easy doesn't mean you should underestimate the subject or the workload. If you do, you will fail," I warn him. He gulps.

The rest of the class consists of me going through the syllabus and answering questions. I don't fail in noticing that Kara didn't bring up her question from earlier. Interesting.

And then class is over.

I watch as all the students rush out the door, probably rushing to get to their next class. It's no secret that the history building is on the completely opposite end of campus from the other buildings and so it takes a while to get to the other buildings from here.

"Ms. Smith," I can't stop myself from calling out just as she is about to walk out the door.

"Yes?"

"I couldn't help but notice you didn't ask your question from earlier," I tell her.

"Oh," she squeaks out, the sound going right to my cock. Fuck. Not now, you.

She looks around, her eyes slightly out of focus and moving rapidly from side to side.

"Are you okay?" I ask her, standing up from my seat. She freezes when I round the table and come to stand right by her. I quickly realize. She's nervous. Why is she so nervous? "Is being around me that bad?"

Her head snaps up to mine.

"Do you think I hate having you around?" she asks and I nod. It's quite obvious. Then she mumbles, "It's the opposite though."

"What?" I'm unsure if I heard her correctly.

Then she looks at me. Properly.

I blink, startled. Why am I so jumpy?

"You want to know why I was there, by your office, waiting for you?" she suddenly asks.

"You had a question about the syllabus," I recall, but she shakes her head.

"I lied," she admits.

"Then why were you there?" I ask.

"Because I wanted to see you," she confesses. "And I couldn't be so shameless to just go see you after breaking things off between us. So, I lied."

I don't say anything, taking it all in.

"I'm sorry," she says, now looking back down. I make sure there are no other students in the hall before making my next move.

Grabbing her chin, I lift it so that she's looking at me again.

"I wanted to see you too," I admit. "But I was hesitant, because I didn't think you'd ever want to see me again."

She chews on her cheek inside her mouth.

"Tell me, Kara," I speak up. "Why did you break things off between us? Why did you tell me to go back to my ex who I don't even want?"

"I thought you deserved better than me," she mumbles, and I almost don't catch it.

"Why in the world would you think that, baby?" I question, reaching for her and pulling her to me. She lets me. "Don't you remember me telling you? You're perfect. For me."

"We still can't be together, anyway," she says, pushing at my chest, but I don't budge. "You're officially my professor now."

"Baby –"

"And I have a date tonight," she cuts in.

What?

"You are not going on that date." I growl.

"You can't tell me what to do." she growls back.

"Then you shouldn't have admitted that you wanted to see me again. That you miss me," I tell her.

"You're right," she says, looking away from me. "I shouldn't have. I made a mistake."

A mistake? Is that what she thinks of what happened between us too?

"I should go," she says, using my distractedness to escape my arms.

And before I know it, she's gone.

CHAPTER 12 – TAKARA

I'm so stupid.

What in the world was I thinking? Oh, right. I wasn't thinking.

I just couldn't help myself. It's been three weeks since I've seen him, and I just wanted to make sure he's okay. After breaking whatever was between us off, I felt guilty, especially after leaving him with that broken look on his face. In that moment, I truly believed I was doing the right thing, for both of us. But after seeing him today, and the way he touched and looked at me, I realize that I may have just been selfish. I mean, I didn't even let him explain himself that day. Maybe I should have. Maybe I should have given him a chance to today. But I didn't. I just walked away after he admitted he's missed me.

And then to make things worse, here I sit now, in a restaurant with a boy, on a date.

I'll admit, he's cute, with his curly blonde locks and chocolate brown eyes. But he's not *him*. I don't mean to compare him to Avery, but it's hard not to, when Avery still consumes my mind, and my heart.

But I'm trying. To forget. To be here, in this moment, with my date.

"So, tell me a bit about yourself," my date, Nathan, says, making an effort to strike up a conversation with me.

"Well, I'm studying history at the university," I say.

"Oh," he says, and I don't fail in noticing the slight disappointment in his voice. I get it. He probably finds it boring, just like most people. "Well, as long as you like it, it doesn't matter what you study."

He flashes me a toothy smile.

"What are you studying?" I ask, taking a sip of my water.

"Law," he answers. "Boring, huh?"

I shake my head, using the same words he did before, "As long as you like it, it doesn't matter what you study."

He smiles, and then suddenly, his eyes darken. It surprises me. Did I do something? No, I don't think so. I mean, he smiled.

"You know what is boring?" he suddenly asks but doesn't wait for me to answer before he answers for me. "This."

Is he referring to our date? I know I haven't put my all into tonight, but surely, I can't be that boring, can I?

"Let's get out of here." he says, not waiting for a response before he stands up and gets his jacket. I wordlessly follow after him.

"Where are we going?" I ask, taking note of the fact that we're not walking to his car. No, we're going in the opposite direction.

"There's a cool club just down the street," he says when I fall in line with him. A club? That doesn't sound like a good idea. But then Zoe's voice rings in my head.

"Don't be scared anymore. You're an adult now. Let loose and put yourself out there. Have fun," she would say to me right now if she were here with me. But she's not here. She's out on a date with her new boyfriend, Derek, so it's not like I can call her to pick me up and ruin her date. She did even mention she was considering spending the night at his place, so that is flown out the window.

I guess my only option is to follow my date into a club and hope he doesn't get too wasted and can't drive me home. I don't live far from campus, but it's far from here.

Nathan leads me to a club called *XXX*, read as Triple X as he says to me. The bouncer lets us in with no problems, and he even high fives Nathan on the way inside.

"I'm a regular here," is all he says to me when he notices my questioning eyes.

Ah. Oh, did I forget to mention that Nathan is twenty-one, two years older than me. But that's nothing to me now, not after –

No. Stop right there. Don't you dare even let yourself think of him. He's off limits, Kara.

"You want a drink?" Nathan shouts over the ear-splitting loud music. I think about saying no, but there's no way I'll be confident to be with him in this moment if I don't have some liquor in me. So I nod and he walks over to the bar without even asking me what I want. Surprise me, I guess.

He shows up by my side minutes later with two beers in his hands. How typical of boys. But I take it anyway, downing a large gulp. Damn, that burns.

"Wanna dance?" he asks me and I'm quick to nod, downing the rest of the beer before handing the empty bottle to him. He smiles, finishing his off too before tossing the empty bottles into the nearby trash can and pulling me onto the dancefloor.

I wrap my arms around his neck and he places his hands on my waist. Safe territory.

We sway from side to side under the music and flashing lights, and I'm surprised when his hands remain rooted on my waist, although, his fingers do squeeze my skin every now and then, like he's itching to touch me more but is waiting for my permission.

Lost in a daze of alcohol, I lean forward, bringing my mouth to his ear and murmuring, "You can touch me, you know?"

He doesn't even hesitate, moving his hands down to my hips. His hands move so frantically, as if he cannot decide where to touch first. I lean my head on his shoulder, letting him figure it out himself. I don't even freeze or tense up when his fingers brush my bare thighs, slowly touching the hem of the skirt Zoe made me wear tonight. I'm not sure whether I like or hate how short it is, especially with him touching me like this.

He's only the second man to touch me like this, but my body reacts as though I've had tons of practice. He pushes his pelvis forward, and I feel something hard against my lower stomach. I gasp at the feeling.

It's not the same as before, but maybe it's better, because this is actually right, and no one will judge me for doing this with *him*.

Then he pulls me up against him, tilting my head back and pressing his mouth to mine. I groan at the contact, tightening my arms around his neck like it's an instinct of mine. His lips are rough and rushed, his tongue seeking mine almost immediately.

I break the kiss, murmuring, "Slow down. We've got all night."

Upon hearing my last words, something sparks in his eyes and a mischievous smile tugs at his lips. Oh, I know what he's expecting now that I've said that. Sex.

I kiss him again, tangling my fingers through his hair. Suddenly, images flash in my mind. Images of a man that's not him, and it spurs me on, makes me bolder.

I press my lower half to his, causing him to groan. I thrust my tongue forward, getting a taste of him. He tastes like that beer he just drank. No, *he* tastes like whiskey, his favourite drink.

He bites my lower lip and I moan, running my fingers over his shoulders and down his muscular arms. Then I trail them up his t-shirt, feeling the hard ridges under my fingertips. He feels so *hard*. I love it.

Then my fingers move down to his jeans, palming him through his pants. He moans over the loud music, pulling at my hair. He's rough, and I like it.

"Avery." I moan. Suddenly, he rips himself away from me. My eyes flutter open, and I snap back to reality. I blink at him while he looks appalled.

"What the fuck did you just call me?" he bursts out, his eyes angry.

"N-Nathan," I lie, my face flushed.

"Then why did I hear you moan another man's name?" he snaps.

"You-you are drunk. It's making you hear things," I tell him. I'm surprised at how steady I'm managing to keep my voice while I'm lying through my teeth.

"I need to leave," he suddenly says and before I can get another word out, he's gone.

Wait. What just happened?

Did he just...ditch me?

Running my fingers through my hair, I turn my body towards the bar and immediately, I find someone's intense stare on me. My heart leaps from my chest when I see who it is.

Avery.

CHAPTER 13 – TAKARA

I'm screwed.

I know immediately.

I am completely and utterly screwed.

Avery gets up from his seat and stalks over to me like a predator, and I'm his prey. I have no doubt he'd enjoy devouring me whole.

I can't deal with this right now.

I turn away from him and head to the door. The bouncer that high-fived Nathan when we got here stops me at the exit/entrance.

"Leaving so soon?" he asks.

"Nathan already left," I grit out before pulling my arm out of his hold and walking out. I don't know how long I walk, but it's only when I can no longer hear the club's music that I stop. It's also now that I realise that I am standing all alone in the main street, the street completely deserted of people and the only company I have are the cars parked on the side of the street.

What was I thinking, just walking out of the club like that, all alone? Well, then, if not alone, who was I supposed to leave with? Avery? No way. Especially not after I imagined it to be him while I was kissing and touching someone else.

I feel awful. I admit, I was a terrible date. I didn't give it my all, and when I finally tried to, I had to think of someone else to get my hypothetical motor running.

Releasing a breath of frustration, I run my fingers through my hair once more. I really didn't want to bother Zoe on her date tonight, but it doesn't look like I have any other choice. But just as I'm about to pull my phone out of my purse, I hear my name being called.

By a voice I know very well.

I turn around, my eyes finding Avery's approaching figure. He looks admittedly intimidating, with his tall figure, all in the dark. But I know better. I know him. He'd never do anything to harm me. I just hope he's not too pissed off by the fact that I kissed someone else.

Wait a minute. He has no right to be pissed off. Whatever we had before is over now. There's no ties between the two of us. If there is anyone who deserves to be pissed off right now, it's Nathan, and he made it perfectly clear that he was, just before he stormed off whilst knowing I have no way home besides him. I'm not really certain whether I can call him selfish or not, because while he ditched me, I'm to blame for it.

"What are you doing out here all alone?" Cameron suddenly snaps. He sounds angry.

"My date ditched me," I lamely say. Honestly, I don't know why I'm telling him this. I should just tell him to leave, to leave me alone, but now that he's here with me, I'm suddenly feeling sorry for myself.

"He what?"

"He left!" I exclaim, then my voice lowers. "It was because of me."

"Oh, I'm sure you did nothing wrong," he says, and the surprising thing is, he sounds like he truly believes that. But it's not like I can tell him the truth about what I did, because that would be humiliating for me.

"Anyway, he left," I say, looking down.

"Do you have a way home?" Avery asks. I shake my head. My actions perplex me. One moment I wanted nothing more than to get away from him, and now that he's here by me, with me, I'm acting completely different. "If you'd let me, I can take you home."

Oh, I know you can, Avery. Is it just going to end with you just dropping me off is the question. Because I'm still hyper aware of how tipsy I am, and although I'm sure he has some sort of self-restraint, I'm not sure I can keep myself from jumping his bones.

"I'm hungry," I suddenly say, looking up at him. Nathan and I left the restaurant before we could order, and I'm feeling it now. But I'm not in the mood for *other* people. "Can we go to a drive-through?"

He smiles, and oh my. My insides melt.

"Whatever you want," he answers, like it's the easiest thing ever. "Let's go. My car is this way."

He leads me back in the direction of the club, and I'm surprised to find his sleek black car parked right in front of the club. How did I not notice it when I arrived here in the first place?

He opens the door for me, like a gentleman, like the gentleman he is, and I get in. He's really not making it any easier for me not to jump his bones right now. He drives to the burger fast food restaurant we came to together before but drives up the drive-through this time. He doesn't even ask me what I want and just orders for me, somehow knowing exactly what I want. He really pays attention. It's one of the things I...like about him.

Once we get our food which he pays for before I can even pull out some cash, he pulls into a parking space in the parking lot and switches off the car.

"You ordered a lot," I note.

"You said you were hungry," he says, taking a long slurp of his strawberry milkshake. I can't take my eyes off his lips that are wrapped around the straw, and suddenly, sinful thoughts creep into my mind. Thoughts of us kissing, and more importantly, of him kissing me where I'm the most sensitive.

Shaking off my thoughts, I shove a few fries into my mouth, but I swallow too quickly that I nearly choke. Avery pats me on the back.

"Careful, baby. We don't want you choking to death, now."

Did he even realise what he just called me?

That pet name truly transforms my ovaries into goo just because it's him saying it.

"I'm okay," I tell him and he stops patting my back and I proceed with my eating. Just like last time, he's done eating before me and even steals a few fries from me. Usually, I hate sharing food. No, always. I always hate sharing my food, especially if you've already gotten your own. But I don't get angry at him. Instead, I just laugh.

Suddenly, it feels like everything is okay between us, like nothing has changed, and in this moment, I don't realise just how dangerous that is. Heck, I wouldn't even protest if he took me back to his place now. In fact, if I wasn't so full, I'd climb onto his lap right now.

Shamelessly.

And he'd like it. I know he would.

"If you're done, shall we go?" he asks and I nod, clicking in my seatbelt. I ignore the disappointment that fills my body when he pulls out of the parking lot. I don't want this night to end just yet. It's been such a long time since we've properly seen one another, in private, and I've missed this. I've missed *him*. But I'm not going to admit that to him. Not again after this morning.

Way too soon, he pulls into my complex's parking lot. But unlike the night of our date, I don't linger in the car with him. In fact, this time, I can't get out of the car soon enough. He gets out too and rounds the car to my side.

"Let me walk you up to your apartment," he offers, but I shake my head.

"It's okay," I say instead of saying what is really in my mind right now. I can't let him be caught bringing me home. Not by my mother. We barely made it out safely last time. Also, according to the college's rules and regulations, professors aren't allowed to be alone with students off campus. And yes, that applies, because he is my professor now. "Well then. Goodnight...Professor."

I walk away before I get to see his reaction to me calling him Professor. I almost said Avery. It was on the tip of my tongue, but that would be inappropriate. Especially since we've finally gotten to a place where we can comfortably be in the same space without touching one another or throwing ourselves at each other.

Maybe, just maybe, we can even be friends. The thought makes me laugh. Never before would I have imagined that I'd be friends with *Avery Wilde*. Then again, never did I think he'd be my professor either. If anything, becoming friends would be the silver lining to this whole thing.

That night, I fall asleep with no dreams of him.

CHAPTER 14 – TAKARA

History is my first class of the day.

As it is my major, I have this class every day. And for the first time, I'm not nervous about it. I'm not nervous about seeing *him*. I've gotten through the last few classes with him, and today should be no different. For the last few classes, we've both completely ignored one another. Like complete strangers. I'm not sure whether I like it or not yet, but what I do know is that I'm a lot relaxed now coming to his class.

I have a smile on my face walking to class, but that fades when I see Nathan standing outside the lecture hall, waiting for me. How does he even know where my class is? Then I realize. Zoe must have told him.

I'm going to choke her when I see her again.

Nathan looks relieved when he sees me. He should be, relieved that I didn't just ignore him, because if he would causes a scene, I know Cameron would sort him out, especially since I'm involved.

"What are you doing here?" I question, folding my arms across my chest.

"I came to apologize," he starts off, but I cut in.

"Only now? Do you realise that the week has almost come to its end and you're only now coming to speak to me?" I scoff.

"You're right. I should have come to you sooner. I was a coward," he admits, and I blink in surprise. I didn't expect him to actually come out and say it. "But I really am sorry. I was drunk that night and it made me hallucinate, hear things that weren't even real. I regret leaving you there that night, and although I know nothing can make up for it, I still want you to know that I'm sorry."

He's stumped me. He's not even using him being drunk as an excuse. Instead, he's admitting he was wrong and is apologizing for it.

"Despite all of that, I like you Kara," he confesses. "And if you'll allow it, I'd like to take you out on a proper date. No clubs or bars. Just us, having a nice dinner or maybe seeing a movie. Your choice."

How do I say no to that? How *can* I say no to that?

"Excuse me," a voice I would never fail to recognize suddenly speaks up. To my side, stands Avery, waiting for Nathan to stop blocking the entrance so that he can walk in.

Did he hear everything?

But before I can read his face to find out if he did, Nathan moves out of the way and he walks inside. My eyes follow him inside, and a feeling of longing wraps around my heart. I really do like him.

Then I turn back to Nathan. Maybe this is my chance, to finally move on from Avery, and maybe even fall for someone new, someone I can actually be with.

"Okay," I say.

"Okay what?" he asks, just to be sure that there is no sort of miscommunication between us.

"Okay, I'll go out with you again. But you promised, no clubs or bars. Just a normal date this time," I say, making myself completely clear this time, and he nods, unable to wipe the smile from his face. Aw, that's cute.

"I'll call you," he says, waving goodbye before walking away. I don't even need to ask him how he got my number. Zoe probably gave it to him. If this date goes well, maybe, just maybe, I won't choke her.

I walk into class and take my usual seat. Just like it's a routine now, Avery completely ignores me unless I ask a question or have an answer to a question, and by the end of the class, I'm nearly out the door when I pause.

Biting my lower lip, I turn around, passing the other students who are leaving and walk right up to his desk. He blinks in surprise when he sees that it's me, but he quickly composes himself as to not give any suspicions to the other students.

When the last student has left the lecture hall, I finally speak, "I need a favour."

"What kind of favour?" he asks, eyeing me closely.

"It's not anything big," I assure him. "It's just...I need some advice."

"About what?"

"A boy."

I wait for his reaction, but he offers me none, the only action he does being blinking. It makes me think to myself. Why did I come to him for advice on Nathan? I could have just asked Zoe. She has plenty of experience when it comes to boys. Why did I put myself and Avery into this situation?

"What about a boy?" he slowly asks.

Then I proceed to tell him about Nathan showing up and apologizing, nothing I'm sure he didn't already hear before since he was there earlier.

"So? What do you think? Did I make a mistake in giving him another chance?" I ask him, pursing my lips in anticipation of his answer.

"Let me ask you something instead, Ms. Smith," he suddenly says, leaning forward on his desk and staring up at me with sharp calculated eyes. "Do you think approaching me regarding this is appropriate?"

My lashes flutter.

Of course it wasn't. I'm so stupid.

"I'm sorry," I immediately apologize. "I made a mistake. It will not happen again. Then I'll get going...sir."

But just as I turn to walk out, he speaks up, "My answer is yes."

"Excuse me?"

"You made a mistake. No *boy* deserves a second chance after doing what he did to a woman like you. Never."

He sounds so sure of himself. A woman like me. Not a girl, but a woman. It makes me smile.

"Thank you for that. You just made me feel very special," I tell him, and he visibly tenses.

"Don't smile," he suddenly snaps.

"What?"

"Don't smile, in front of me. Unless you are willing to bear the consequences," he warns me.

My smile slowly fades.

"What consequences?" I'm brave enough to ask.

His pupils dilate.

Then he stands up, quite abruptly.

"Tell me Ms. Smith. No, Takara. Would you like to be friends with me?" he asks.

"Friends...?" I slowly blink.

"Since we can't be lovers, I've decided that the only logical thing to do is become friends," he says.

"Logical?" I ask. "What about what you just asked me was logical?"

"Just answer the question," he shrugs my question off. "Do. You. Want. To be. My friend?"

"I do," I say before I even realise what's coming out of my mouth.

A smile tugs at his lips.

"Okay then."

I just stare at him.

"From today onwards, the two of us are friends."

Somehow, this sounds like a very bad idea.

CHAPTER 14 – AVERY

Why did I ask Kara to be my friend?

Why didn't I just continue ignoring her like I have all week?

Oh, right. Because I can't stop thinking about her. Because she consumes every fibre of my mind and body. She haunts me when I'm awake and when I'm asleep. When I see her, and look at her full lips, all I can imagine is her wrapping those lips around my cock and sucking me dry. And in my dreams, I'm tasting her, eating her out like a hungry animal, savouring her sweet taste. Kara tastes like champagne to me. I should have told her that before.

It's inappropriate for me to tell her now. Then she'd know I've been thinking about her like that, still.

I adjust myself in my pants before my next class starts.

Students filter in and takes their seats and within minutes, I'm starting the class. This class goes more smoothly, especially since there's no vixen here to distract me.

When class is over, a female student stops by my desk, smiling brightly at me. She has a blinding smile, and I resist the urge to squint.

"How may I help you?"

"I'm a fan!" she yells out, holding out a copy of the 1st year history textbook in front of her. "Could you please sign this for me?"

I blink in surprise.

"A...fan?" I repeat. I wasn't even aware I had fans. "But why?"

"What do you mean why?" she laughs. "You're handsome. And the youngest professor on campus."

I blink once more.

I had no idea I have...fans.

"Are you sure you want me to sign that? I mean, once I sign it, you won't be able to sell it afterwards," I tell her.

"Why in the world would I sell it?" She looks horrified at the mere thought of it. "Having you sign it makes it the most valuable thing I own."

"The most valuable thing you own...huh," I mutter under my breath. I'm still not sure I understand this, but I take the textbook from her and sign it before handing it back to her, however, instead of taking the book, she grabs onto my forearms.

"Your tattoos are really cool," she gushes, her eyes so big I have to wince.

"Thank you," I say, trying to pull myself out of her grip, but she just holds on tighter. Of course if I want to, I can easily get myself loose, but I might end up hurting her with my strength or end up pulling her across the desk and onto me. That'll just give her the wrong idea.

"Can you tell me about them?" she asks.

"There's not much to say," I say and, in her disappointment, her grip loosens, allowing me to break free. I keep my hands at my sides, not wanting to give her another opportunity to touch me. "If that's all, I need to prepare for my next class."

I actually don't have another class until late this afternoon, but she doesn't have to know that.

Her face falls at me dismissing her, but she quickly plasters a fake smile on her face, offering me a wave before *finally* leaving.

I spend the rest of my day in peace with loose thoughts of a certain brunette.

CHAPTER 15 – TAKARA

I glare at Zoe.

She sifts through my entire closet, tossing possible options behind her, some even hitting me in the face.

"Why are you doing this?" I groan, catching a top in my hands.

"Getting you an outfit," she simply says.

"Exactly, why? I believe I told you I don't want to go," I remind her.

"That's because you've never been, so you only think you don't want to, but trust me, you want to," she tells me. I'm really not appreciating the gaslighting happening here.

Zoe heard about a frat party and has been convincing me to go with her for the past hour but considering the fact that she's still searching for an outfit for me, I'd say my no's have fallen on deaf ears.

"Look," she starts off, finally walking away from my closet and coming to stand in front of me. "I know that this is out of your comfort zone, but I'll be there the entire time. Besides, Nathan is going to be there too."

"And that's supposed to put me at ease?" I retort.

"Of course," she says, staring at me with confused. "Listen, he likes you so he'll take care of you tonight."

I hate how nice that sounds. I've never had someone take care of me before.

Eh-wrong. Avery took care of you, my subconscious reminds me.

That he did.

And then I realise exactly what I should do.

"Fine. Let's go. To that party," I say and Zoe cheers. After another fifteen minutes of her sorting out my clothes, we finally have an outfit that we can both approve of. A high-waisted skinny jean with a cropped lacy black top.

I apply some mascara and a lip gloss and then we're on our way to the party. It's being held at a guy named Noah's house, and when we arrive, I'm left gaping. This guy lives in a mansion.

"You know what, I change my mind about Nathan," Zoe suddenly says. "You should go for Noah instead."

"Money is not everything, Zoe," I practically preach.

"Yeah, because if it was to you, you'd be dripping wet for Noah right now."

I'm not even fazed by her words. I'm used to how vulgar she can be already. So, instead of responding, I grab her arm and pull her to the house. When we walk in, we're instantly surrounded by people, complete strangers, all with red paper cups in their hands that I assume has alcohol in it.

Nathan appears out of nowhere.

"Kara! You look so hot tonight," he purrs, his hands coming to sit on my hips. I can smell the hint of beer on his breath. So not attractive.

When he leans in to kiss me, I turn my head, causing his lips to land on my cheek. He laughs, wrapping an arm around my shoulders.

"Let's get you something to drink," he says and leaves no room for protest because he immediately drags me to the bar and leaving Zoe behind. I turn my head to look for her, but she's already gone. I wonder if Derek is here. Would a guy his age attend a frat party? I'm not sure since I don't know him. Heck, I've never even met the guy.

Three drinks later, I'm tipsy and somehow end up on the couch, on Nathan's lap. He's no better than me, his eyes half-closed.

People have now just started forming a circle to play never have I ever.

"Shall we go upstairs?" Nathan mumbles in my ear but I shake my head.

"Let's play a game," I say, flashing him a drunk smile. My face feels so warm right now, I'm surprised it's not itchy.

"Okay. So you all know the rules. Start!" the only sober person in the room says.

I lean back against Nathan's chest. His fingers distract me from the game, trailing up my denim-clad thighs. It's kind of ticklish, and I giggle.

"I hate these jeans." He groans, and I laugh. Of course it does. It prevents him from touching my bare skin. I can take them off, but that sounds like too much of a hassle right now.

Then I look down, and I start giggling.

"You're hard, Nathan." I giggle, throwing my head back. Immediately, his lips latch onto my exposed neck, and I gasp in surprise. He licks my skin, before starting to suckle on it. I moan, before pushing him away so that I can sit up.

I touch my hand to my neck where he kissed me, surprised to find it feeling very sensitive. But I can hardly care what that means right now. Instead, I lean forward and kiss him.

I like kissing him. He's a good kisser, and the alcohol really does help. He cups the back of my head with his hand, tilting my head so that he can deepen the kiss. I moan in response.

"Get a room you two!" someone yells out and then I feel a pillow hit me. I break the kiss with a frown.

"You heard the man," is all Nathan says before standing up with me in his arms and starts walking up the stairs. I hide my face in his neck. I know exactly where we're headed. There are only bedrooms and bathrooms up here, so unless he has to pee, I know exactly what's going to happen. This is probably the point where I stop him, but I don't want to. I want to see where this leads. I want to see how I feel when he touches me, when he puts his mouth on me.

I want to know if it will feel as good as it was with...with who now again?

I can't seem to remember.

Nathan carries me into an empty bedroom and throws me onto the bed. I giggle, splaying my arms out above my head. I hear the pop of a button, and then soon, my jeans are being pulled down my legs. I shiver at the coldness that wraps around my bare legs, but when I want to pull them up, Nathan pulls them back down. I can't see anything. I can only feel while I stare at the white ceiling.

Nathan crawls in between my legs and smells me, inhaling me through my underwear.

"You smell so good," he murmurs before placing a wet kiss on the material. I arch my back off the bed, trying to feel something, anything. But I'm as dry as a Sahara down there, and Nathan notices. So he tries harder. He parts my panties, revealing me to him bare. When his tongue touches me, I squirm. And when his tongue thrusts into me, I scream.

Why does it suddenly hurt so much?

Then the bedroom door flies open and someone comes barging in.

"You asshole!" the person yells out before coming to my side. "Kara. Kara, open your eyes."

I only manage to open my eyes halfway so the person above me is blurry, but I recognize the voice.

"Zoe." I sniffle. She embraces me.

"It's okay. It's all going to be okay, Kara," she assures me.

But it's not.

This night is ruined.

CHAPTER 16 – TAKARA

I feel sick.

And that's why the first thing I did after waking up was come to the campus café and order me an espresso, black, with no sugar. The bitterness should be able to wake me up, because I've got a class later, a history class that I cannot afford to miss because we're getting our term assignment explained today. I meant to read through the material last night, but thanks to Zoe, I ended up at a frat party and nearly ended up losing my virginity to a guy who cared more about the fact that he was horny than the fact that I was completely out of it.

I'll admit, he didn't *exactly* take advantage of me, but he should have known better. I thought he was more respectful than that. Luckily Zoe stormed in there. Otherwise...God. I don't even want to think about it.

The café is completely packed, and I was lucky to grab the last open table. But unfortunately, someone else was not so lucky.

"You're Kara, right?" an unfamiliar voice speaks up. I turn my head, my eyes landing on who I'm assuming is another student with a lean figure, but bulbous calves. He must be a jock. He runs his fingers through his chestnut-coloured hair before taking a seat opposite me. "I can sit, right?"

Well, you're already sitting so...

But I keep my mouth shut, just offering him a tight smile.

"I've been looking for you all morning, and I finally found you," he tells me.

"*You* were looking for...me?" I ask and he nods. "If you don't mind me asking, who are you?"

"I'm Conan. Nathan's best bud," he says and something in me sinks. Of course he is.

I don't bother with faking my smile anymore.

"But why were you looking for me?" I ask him, trying my best to be polite.

"Nathan wants me to deliver a message," he informs. "He says sorry about last night."

The way he says it, he's belittling what happened last night.

"I don't appreciate your tone, *Conan*," I grit out.

"What tone?" he asks, looking around him as if people are listening to us. Why would they? "I'm merely a messenger. If you have a problem with the way I say things, that's your thing."

"Exactly," I agree. "Why are you the one sitting here at this table with me and not Nathan?"

"He's hungover. Has a split aching headache," he distractedly says.

"Then he could have called," I state.

"Women are so much work," he mutters under his breath, but I hear him clearly.

"What?"

"Why don't you just accept the apology and move on?" he suggests. "No way. You don't really think you were taken advantage of last night, do you?"

"Then what was that? I was clearly out of it. I could barely keep my eyes open but your *friend* still decided to take off my pants," I say.

"And that's *all* he did," he suddenly exclaims, like he's fed up with me. "Jesus. All he did was touch you a little. But you screamed like you were being raped."

Now people are looking at us.

"Lower your voice."

"Why? Are you scared? That people will find out what a slut you are?!" he yells out, completely on purpose. I blink rapidly, willing him to stop talking.

"Please. Stop," I mumble a soft plead.

"Admit it Kara. You wanted it. You kissed him first. You let me him touch you. You seduced him. And then when things got too much for you, you screamed bloody murder."

By the time he's done, my eyes are filled with tears. Everyone heard him. Everyone in the café.

"Why are you doing this? What did I ever do to you?"

"You framed my best friend," he says, his voice dark.

"I didn't do any of the sort!" I abruptly stand up. I'm the one yelling now, but I can't keep it in.

"You did," he says, rising to his feet after me. "You wanted him to touch you. You ached for his tongue to touch you there. Then you decided oops. You don't want it anymore? Too bad. You already consented. So, you should have just laid there and taken it like the slut that you are."

I fall. Hitting the ground.

"Stop." I cry out, burying my face in my hands.

"What did you just call her?" a deadly voice speaks up. I know that voice. It takes everything in me to look up from my hands, my heart stuttering in my chest when I see Avery standing beside me, but in front of Conan. He *towers* over Conan, and if you don't know him like I do, he's very intimidating.

"Professor, this has nothing to do with you so I suggest you leave." Conan says. Avery chuckles. It's dark. Sinister.

"Who are you? Who are you to tell *me* what to do? Who are you to call *her* a slut? How dare you?!" he roars. Conan flinches.

"Why are you even butting in here?" Conan yells out, but it's faux confidence. I can see it in his eyes. His eyes tell the truth. He's *scared*.

"Ms. Smith is *my* student which gives me the right to protect her from these kinds of situations," Avery says, deadly calm all of a sudden.

"You mean situations such as her sex life?"

Avery is the one who flinches this time, but not because he's scared. No, there's something else lingering in his eyes. Hurt.

"That's quite inappropriate, don't you think, *Professor*?" He's throwing that title in Avery's face.

"Stop," I mumble but neither of them seem to hear me.

"What's inappropriate is you exposing intimate details of Ms. Smith's private life in front of everyone," Avery says, gesturing to the people surrounding us. "Or...was that your intention from the beginning?"

"I wouldn't have started this if that bitch just shut her trap and listened to me," he snaps, glowering down at me.

Avery steps forward, now standing in front of me fully.

"Don't call her that."

"Or what?" Conan challenges Avery.

Avery chuckles, "Consider yourself lucky that as a professor, I'm not allowed to touch you."

Conan gulps. Avery leans forward, until his mouth is by Conan's ear and whispers something to him, so softly, only Conan can hear it and no one, not even me, can. All the blood drains from Conan's face almost immediately. Then Avery steps away from him and turns to face me before leaning down on his knees in front of you.

"Do you think you can stand?" he asks me, and although I'm not one hundred percent sure I can without my legs giving in, I nod. I have to try. Avery grabs my hand and helps me up, but just as I stand upright, my legs buckle and I'm falling once again, only this time, Avery is here to catch me, his arm wrapping around me in a protective manner. I lean against his side, closing my eyes.

His natural body scent is calming, and I breathe it in.

"Can I touch you?" His question has my eyes fluttering open. "Just until I can get you out of here."

Instead of using words, I just reach up and wrap my arms around his neck. He takes this as a yes and reaches down, scooping me into his arms until he's carrying me. I hide my face in his neck, hating all the stares and let him carry me out of the café. I'm not sure how long we walk, but I only open my eyes when he stops.

We are standing beside his car, parked in the staff's parking lot with a special sign reserved just for Professor Wilde.

"I didn't know where to take you on campus," he stars explaining. "So, I was thinking I could take you home."

"But mom is there and mom can't see me like this –" I cut myself off when I realise. My mother works here. "Dammit. My mom is going to find out everything. This is all so messed up."

"No, she won't. I'll take care of it," Cameron assures me.

"How?" I ask.

"Let me worry about that," he says. "But for now, let's get you into my car because it might stir up some extra trouble if we keep standing here like this."

He gestures to us. Him carrying him. Me in his arms. Student and Professor. Right. Completely wrong.

I nod, letting him place me into the car. I relax against the leather seat, releasing a breath of relief.

"Wait," I suddenly say when he's inside the car. "What about class?"

"I'll cancel," he says, as if its as simple as that.

"You can't just –"

"I said I'll cancel," he cuts me off, offering me a reassuring smile. So, I nod in defeat. If he says he will take care of everything, why should I make things unnecessarily difficult for myself?

Avery starts the engine and starts driving.

"What did you tell Conan before we left?" I can't help but ask him. It's been on my mind ever since I saw Conan's reaction.

"Nothing," he shrugs.

"It can't have been nothing," I argue. Then suddenly, his hand lands on my thigh and he squeezes my flesh.

"Nothing for you to worry about," he says, sparing me a glance through the mirror, however, my eyes are glued to his hand on my thigh. Does he not realise that it's there? Does he not realise how wrong this is?

I know, but I don't make any move to remove his hand. Instead, I place my hand on top of his and squeeze. He doesn't say anything or react in any way, so I don't move my hand away. It stays there throughout the entire ride to my home.

"Don't go," I say when he parks in my complex parking lot. "Please."

I don't think I can be alone right now.

He smiles softly.

"I wasn't planning on going anywhere," he assures me, letting go of his hold on me and causing my hand to slip off his to get out of the car. He rounds the car quickly, coming to open my door for me and holding a hand out to me.

He's being so thoughtful. It has my heart melting in my chest.

So, I take his hand and let him pull me up and out of the car. Then suddenly, he's picking me up into his arms again, and I squeal in surprise, but my arms automatically move to wrap around his neck.

"I think I can walk now," I tell him, although, I secretly don't want him to let me go. I want to stay in his arms, for as long as I can, for as long as he'll allow me.

He shakes his head.

"I'm carrying you." He says it as a matter of fact.

I try to hide my smile, but I fail miserably. So I just opt to hide my face in his neck so that he can't see me. He just laughs, before starting to walk. He carries me all the way up to my apartment – luckily there's an elevator – and when we reach the door, I blindly hand him the keys to unlock it.

I don't know how he manages, but he manages to open the door whilst still holding me in his arms. Then he carries me inside, flicking on the living room/kitchen's light. He carries me to the kitchen counter, right next to the refrigerator.

I reluctantly let him go, but as if he too cannot stop touching me, he keeps his hands planted firmly on my waist.

"Are you hungry?" he asks me, nodding to the refrigerator. I want to shake my head no, but then I remember I had nothing today besides a few sips of that espresso.

"I could eat," I say and he nods, his hands leaving me as he steps in front of the refrigerator and pulls it open. There's not much of anything in there, I can see from here, just a few water bottles, some bread and cheese.

"Is grilled cheese okay?" he asks. I nod excitedly. Grilled cheese is my favourite.

He makes work of making me that sandwich, easily finding his way around our tiny kitchen.

"Is your mom going to do the shopping today?" he asks, referring to the basically empty refrigerator. I shrug. She's usually too tired after work. "Then what will you eat for dinner tonight?"

I shrug again, and he frowns. I've never really thought much of this. I usually just eat whatever there is, and if there's nothing, I just go to bed hungry. It's not as bad it seems. It's the reason why I've managed to stay somewhat in shape.

He's quiet as he finishes off my grilled cheese and when it's done, my mouth waters. He hands it to me on a plate and blows on it a few times so that it's not too hot for me. I can't help but smile at the small yet so sweet gesture.

Then I dig in and within a few less bites than I would have liked in front of him, it's up.

I smile sheepishly at him when I catch his eyes on me, a small smile playing on his lips.

"Nice?" he asks, and I nod. Better than.

He takes the plate from me, and despite my protests, he proceeds to wash it out on the sink.

"Stay," is all he said, and I listened. Like a good girl.

Then when he's done, he returns to me and places his hands back on my waist, like they belong there. Foolishly, I think maybe they do. Then he becomes serious.

"Are you okay?"

My smile fades. I know what he's referring to.

"I'm okay," I say, looking down. "I just wish it didn't happen...in front of...*you*."

I feel like my dirty secret has been aired and Avery, the last person I wanted to find out, found out.

"Why me?" he asks, his eyebrows furrowing.

"Because of...you know...what...ever we were," I mumble, unable to look up at him. It's not fair. Even up here on the counter, he's still taller than me.

"But we're friends now, aren't we?"

My eyes lift to his.

"Really? You really mean that?" I ask him.

"I'll admit, hearing those things were hard. That night at the club, when you were with that guy, kissing him and letting him touch you, that was hard for me too," he admits, and it makes my heart hurt. "But I made a decision that night too. That I'd be your friend, someone who would here for you when you needed them."

So, he's basically saying he likes me but decided to be my friend instead because it's what he thinks I need from him?

"I...I didn't do those things with him because I wanted to," I admit, pursing my lips when he frowns. "To be honest, the only reason why I did it was because I wanted to forget about you...and feel something for someone else."

He's silent.

"But...it didn't work," I continue. "I couldn't feel anything. I wasn't aroused. I didn't want him to touch me. I just...convinced myself into doing it, hoping that at some point, things would change."

"But that didn't work," he finishes off for me, and I nod. "Now, tell me, and be honest."

I nod, bracing myself for his question.

"What do you want from me?"

"I want you to be my boyfriend."

There. I said it. It's out there. No takebacks now.

"You've been through a lot, Kara," he starts off, and I know what's coming. "And although I want the same thing, a boyfriend is not what you need right now."

A rejection.

But he's doing it for my sake, so I can't even be mad at him.

Tears prick my eyes. He notices immediately, reaching up to cup my face in his hands.

"Don't cry," he says, wiping away a fallen tear. "I'll still be here for you. Just not as a lover, but...as a friend."

I launch myself at him, wrapping myself around him. He hugs me back, holding me to him as I work through all my emotions. I feel hurt and sad, but I know that he's right. After what happened with Nathan, I realised that I'm not ready to be in a relationship yet.

"Don't leave me," I say into his shoulder.

"I'm not going anywhere," he promises. "I'll be right here when you need me."

I don't let go of him, because right now, I need this.

I need him.

CHAPTER 17 – TAKARA

Avery brought me shopping.

I told him he doesn't have to, but he insisted, and if there's something I've realised, it's that he doesn't back down from anything. That, and the fact that I can't say no to him.

And so, fifteen minutes later, I find myself going down aisle after aisle with Avery behind me, pushing the trolley.

I grab all the essentials which in its entirety is only more bread and cheese. Then I turn back to Avery.

"I'm done. We can go now," I say but just as I want to turn around, he grabs my arm and pulls me back. "What?"

"You only grabbed exactly what you have at home right now. How can you be done?" he questions, his eyes surprisingly stern.

"I'm not a big eater," I lie.

"Don't lie to me, Takara. I've seen you eat. Remember?" he reminds me, and I purse my lips, not saying anything. "So, if you decide you're done, I'll just have to start."

"What?" I blurt out, but he doesn't pay attention to me. Instead, he pushes the trolley down the aisle, grabbing whatever he wants to and tossing it inside. "You can't do this."

"Why not?" he challenges. "Clearly, you are not willing to do this properly, so I'll just have to do it for you."

Pursing my lips, I follow him around the store like a lost puppy. But when he grabs the third kind of cereal, I place my hand on his arm, stopping him.

"That's enough now," I tell him, gesturing to the full trolley.

"Is there anything else you may need?" he asks but I shake my head. He's already covered everything and then more. I stare at all the things he grabbed. That's got to be groceries for a whole month, well, at least it is in my household. He also chose the best quality things, meaning that it's the most expensive. I'm not even sure if I'll be able to pay for all of this.

Staring up at Avery who stares down at me with a frown, I realise that he was just doing what he thinks is best for me. I'd feel too bad to put some things back. Clutching my purse in my hand, I pray I have enough to pay for all of this as I walk to the front counter.

Avery does the honours of packing everything out while I keep my eyes on the register. The balance is rising rapidly, and by the time everything is checked out, my eyes are wide. I definitely don't have enough for that. But just as I want to tell the cashier to take out the ridiculously expensive cereal, Avery is sliding his card into the card machine.

"No!" I exclaim, grabbing his arm. "What do you think you're doing?"

"Paying," he simply says.

"No!" I exclaim once more. "It's my groceries. Why would you pay?"

"Because we're friends," he says, as if it's obvious.

"Is this your first time being someone's friend?" I ask him, staring at him incredulously.

"No," he says. "But it is my first time being friends with someone I have feelings for. So, what's the protocol?"

I blink at him. Did he just...yes he did. He just admitted to having feelings for me. I mean, I always knew, but him actually *saying* it confirms it on a whole other level for me.

"Kara?"

I blink out of it.

"Protocol, right," I mutter. "It means that I pay for my things. You don't get to just pay because you feel like it anymore."

"Can I ask you a favour and promise you won't get mad?" he asks, and I nod, albeit reluctantly. "If I want to do something, you'll let me. No questions asked."

"That hardly seems fair," I tell him.

"That's why it's a favour," he says.

"I'm not sure. It sounds like it can work out to be quite dangerous for me," I note.

"Don't worry. I won't use it to take advantage of you. Just for little things, like this."

I wasn't thinking he would take advantage of me, though.

"Okay," I agree. "I'll do you this favour."

"Great," he pipes out, a smile coming to his face. "Which means I'll be paying."

The triumphant expression on his face says I've been stumped. So, I just stand there, letting him pay for my groceries. Now that I think about it, we've eaten together three times, all of which he has paid for. I haven't paid for a thing when we're together since I've met him. I make a mental vow to pay for whatever meal we share together next. I don't tell him though, because he'll make extra sure that doesn't happen.

"Want to eat out tonight?" Avery asks as we walk out of the store, plastic bags in hand. Of course, he's carrying all of them, letting me hold onto only the chocolate bar he bought me. He's such a gentleman, and I'm afraid if I spend too much time in his company, I'll get spoiled.

"You mean, the two of us? Together?" I ask him and he nods. "I don't know about that..."

We have broken one of the biggest rules today. The two of us, professor and student, are *alone* together, with no supervision. The longer we stay in each other's company, the more likely we are to be caught together.

"If you're worried about people seeing us, we can go someplace out far, or we can even go to a drive through and eat in the car," he offers, and although, that sort of solves our problem, I'm still unsure about this. We've basically spent the entire day so far together. Isn't that enough for *just* friends? "Okay, let me just take you home and then I'll get out of your hair."

He hurriedly loads the groceries in his car, but I rush over to him, grabbing his arm.

"Are you angry?" I ask him, my voice soft. He can't be angry at me. I don't like it.

"I'm not angry," he says, although the look on his face tells me otherwise. "I just know when to take a hint."

A hint. I guess I was giving him the hint that this was enough already.

The car ride to my apartment complex is silent and awkward. I want to do something, say something to lighten the mood, but I have no idea what. Then we pull up into the parking lot, and I fear it's too late.

"Are you busy tomorrow?" I ask him once he's turned the car off.

"Tomorrow?" he repeats, and I nod. "No. Why?"

"Then, will you let me cook for you?"

He blinks, not quite understanding where I'm going with this.

"After classes tomorrow, you can come over for dinner. I'll cook."

"What about your mom?" he asks.

"She's never home during the weekend. Always stays with friends."

"And leaves you alone?" When I nod, a frown creases his face. "I don't like that."

"It's okay. I'm a big girl," I tell him.

"It doesn't matter," he says, the frown still evident on his face. "There are some crazy people out there."

I smile.

"Why are you smiling?" he questions.

"It's the first time, someone cared so much about me-my safety," I say, staring up at him with shy eyes.

"Well, you'd better get used to it," he says, leaning forward. "Because I'm not going anywhere."

I smile wider.

"Good," I agree. "I don't want you to go anywhere either."

He smiles.

It's true. Whether he be my lover or just my friend, I don't want him leaving my life. Ever.

CHAPTER 18 – AVERY

Why the hell am I so nervous?

Oh, right. It's because I'm going on a date with Kara. No, wait. We're just friends, so I can't call it a date. This is just the two of us, hanging out as friends. Friends who don't touch, who don't kiss. This is going to be a great night.

Wow, who the hell am I kidding? I sound like a liar, even to my own ears.

Friends. What a stupid concept. That's the last thing I would call us. If anything, what we have is a situation-ship, not just friends, but not quite lovers.

I'll have to control myself tonight. I have to put a friendly smile on my face and do my best to pretend I don't imagine her naked every single time I look at her. I've basically seen everything about her, besides her breasts, but I know those will be a sight to see too.

What do I wear tonight? I can't dress too formal because then she'd think I think it's a date, but I can't dress too casually or she'll think I don't care about looking good for her, and that's the thing. I *want* to look good for her.

God, I feel like such a girl right now, fussing over what to and not to wear. I bet she wouldn't care. She already likes me enough to care. Or, at least I think so. As far as I'm aware of, she hasn't dated since, well, whatever you could call us. That boy, Nathan was the first.

Just thinking about that night at the club makes my blood boil. I'm not even sure what I was doing there. I mean, what respectable thirty-year-old professor goes to clubs?

They kissed that night. He touched her. I hated that, but I couldn't look away. And then the bastard ditched her, fully knowing she had no other way home. Then I think to yesterday. What his friend said.

I breathe in deeply,

Don't think about that. Don't think about his lips on hers. Don't think about his hands on her. Don't think about his tongue on her –

Fuck. Before I realise it, my hands are clenched into fists.

I shouldn't get angry. I know I have no right to. But I can't help it. Kara is *mine*, whether we're dating or not. It's just a label anyway. What really matters is how we feel about one another.

And in my heart, she's mine.

*****

I arrive at Kara's apartment and knock on the door.

Okay, Avery. You're going to control yourself tonight. Yes, you two will be all alone in her apartment tonight, but you can do this. You can hold back. You can *not* act on your urges and desires. Why? Because this is not what she needs right now.

What she needs right now is a friend. So, I have to be that for her. Otherwise, I have no place in her life.

The door opens.

My breath hitches when I lay my eyes on her. She didn't put much thought into her outfit. In fact, she's dressed for the house, in her denim shorts, mickey mouse sweater, and her matching slippers. Her hair is pulled up in a simple bun and her face is bare, stripped of any makeup she may have worn throughout the day.

She's beautiful.

"You look...handsome. I should probably have dressed up properly too."

She looks embarrassed, but I shake my head.

"You look perfect," I say, handing her the singular red rose I bought on the way here. She smiles and invites me in. She disappears into her room for a few moments and then returns.

"It smells good in here," I tell her, and it's true. It really does smell divine.

"I hope it tastes as good as it smells," she sheepishly says.

She's nervous, I realise. So, I'm not the only one. Does it make me a bad person for being glad?

"We don't have a dining room table, so I hope you don't mind eating on the couch," she says.

"Doesn't matter to me." As long as we're together. In fact, it might be better this way, because this way, I get to sit next to her instead of opposite her. Silver linings.

I sit down on the couch and watch Kara as she dishes food into two plates, my mouth watering. I wasn't hungry before coming here, but I definitely am now.

She carries the two plates in her tiny hands and hands one to me. There's so much food, from homemade fried chicken to coleslaw, and my favourite, mashed potatoes.

I dig in to the mash first, groaning in delight when I taste it on my tongue.

"Is it okay?" Kara timidly asks. I turn to her with big eyes.

"Okay? It's better than okay. This might be the best mash I've ever had."

She blushes at the compliment, a shy smile present on her face before she starts eating too. I gobble up the food like its my last meal, and when I'm done, I'm completely satisfied with a full belly. Kara is done shortly after me and takes our plates to the kitchen. I offer to wash the dishes, but she insists on doing them herself, especially since I'm her 'guest'.

So, while she's busy, I switch on the TV and scroll through the channels. They don't have as many channels as I do, but luckily, they have Netflix. Kara joins me back on the couch soon and I hand her the remote.

"You choose," I tell her.

"But you're the guest," she reminds me. I want to protest, but then I get an idea.

"Then...horror?" I ask and she nods, handing me the remote. I try to gauge her reaction, but she offers none, her face a blank canvas. Looks like my plan failed. I was hoping she's scared of horror movies and would snuggle up to me during the movie, but I guess that's not happening.

Pouting in dejection, I press play on the first horror movie that pops up.

We are completely silent as the movie plays, the only sounds being our breathing. Then I realise, turning my body to Kara. She's breathing quite heavily.

"Are you okay?" I ask her, and she nods, although the sweat forming on her forehead tells me otherwise. "Is it the movie? Should I stop it?"

She shakes her head.

"You're my guest and you wanted to watch this, so, we'll watch it."

A smile tugs at my lips. She's indeed not good with horror movies. No, she's terrified, and we haven't even gotten to the scary parts yet.

I switch off the TV completely. Then I scoot over to her, until my body is pressed against her side.

"What-what are you doing?" she stammers, and I smile at her red tinted cheeks.

I reach out to tuck a stray strand of hair behind her ear.

"Are you scared?" I ask her. She gulps but doesn't answer. "Want me to hold you?"

"No!" she bursts out, her face like a ripe tomato.

"You're incredibly cute, you know that?" I murmur, gently stroking her face with my fingers.

Then she turns to me with serious eyes.

"What are you doing? I thought we're only friends."

I blink. She's right. What was I doing? Why did I touch her? After promising her I wouldn't.

"I'm sorry," I immediately apologize. "I wasn't thinking."

I really wasn't.

"You know I like you," she suddenly confesses. "But you were the one who drew the line. The one who said we can only be friends. So, unless you are planning on taking it all the way, don't give me false hopes."

She said other things, but my mind stopped working after she said take it all the way. Does she want me to take it all the way? Is she ready for that?

Clearly, she is, otherwise she wouldn't have said that.

I want to take things all the way with you too, is on the tip of my tongue, but it doesn't come out. Instead, I say, "Want to come home with me?"

She blinks in surprise.

So I backtrack.

"It's just...I'm not comfortable with leaving you here all alone is all," I try to explain, but my words come out in a spluttering mess.

Then Kara bursts out laughing.

"What? Was that that funny?" I feel embarrassed, and trust me, this never happens. "Do you find me funny?"

"No. No, I wasn't laughing at you," she tries to make up, but I look away with a huff. Yes, I'm aware that I'm being extremely childish right now, but its honestly just so that I can see what she does next. "Really. I wasn't laughing at you, but *with* you."

"Was I laughing?"

Her face sobers, and immediately, I feel bad.

"Hey. It's okay. I'm –"

"It's because you're cute!" she cuts in.

What? Did she just...?

"You think I'm cute? You're even cuter. Way way cuter!" she exclaims, a determined look on her face. I smile.

I pull her to me, wrapping my arms around her small form.

"I have a Jacuzzi at my place. Want to try it out?"

Even I don't know what I'm suggesting. Will she think I want to fuck her in my Jacuzzi? Do I want to? Heck yeah. That'd be so hot.

Kara's body flushes and her pupils dilate.

"Yes," she surprises me by saying. "Let's try it out. Us."

I twitch it my pants.

"Now go pack. You're not coming back here tonight," I tell her, and she nods, jumping off the couch and disappearing into her room.

I adjust myself in my pants, a satisfied smirk on my face.

I have a feeling tonight is going to be very interesting.

And hot.

CHAPTER 19 – TAKARA

Nerves bubble within me.

Here I stand, in Avery's bathroom, half naked, staring at myself in the mirror. He left me here to change and get ready for the Jacuzzi. I've been here for a solid fifteen minutes. I'm surprised he hasn't knocked yet. If I were him, I'd think I chickened out. I'm almost there, especially as I stare at the bikini on my body.

This is my sexiest bikini, all red and lace, matching. I'm not even sure what possessed me to pick this one from my closet. I have plenty of conservative one-pieces in my closet. I've never even wore this one before, and for good reason. It's *very* revealing, the lace not doing much to hide *anything*. I can even see my nipples right through the thin material.

I can change, say I changed my mind and have him drive me home. But I don't want to. There's a reason why this bikini set spoke to me when I opened that drawer. Its because after the way Cameron looked at me, all thoughts of us being *just* friends flew out the window.

Now, we're just two individuals who are very much attracted to one another.

I look at myself once more.

If I wear this, there is really no hiding any part of me. He'll see *everything*.

But I want that, don't I? The thought of him seeing me in this makes me all fluttery, and excited.

Then the knock comes.

"You okay in there?"

"I'll be right out," I yell out and then I hear his footsteps retreating.

You can do this, Takara. You want this. You want *him*.

Grabbing a fluffy white towel from the rack, I wrap it around myself before walking out of the bathroom. He's standing all ready at the Jacuzzi, waiting for me when I arrive. It's on is balcony, meaning we have the view of the entire city.

I clear my throat, catching his attention.

"Come here," he says, his eyes fixed on me as he holds out his hand to me. I walk to him, taking his hand. His free hand comes up to the part keeping the towel together. "Let's get rid of this, shall we?"

Then he tugs it loose, and the towel falls at my feet.

His breath hitches as his eyes graze over every inch of me, slowly, as if committing my body to memory.

"Fuck," he curses. "You look so beautiful, baby."

Baby.

Then he groans, as if he's in pain.

"Let's get in."

I let him lead me into the Jacuzzi and let go of his hand so I can go to the opposite end of it. I lean my back against it, the water coming just above my breasts. He watches me through lidded eyes, his blue eyes almost completely black.

"Why are you so far away?"

Because I'm nervous. Its highly likely that tonight is *the* night. The night I lose my virginity. He doesn't even know that I'm a virgin. At some point, I'm going to have to tell him. Just, not yet.

"Come to me," he says, beckoning me to him. I let my body lead me, right into his arms.

I gasp when his hands land on my waist, his fingers squeezing my flesh.

"What are we doing?" I can't help but ask. This might ruin the entire mood, but I have to ask.

"Relaxing," he answers.

"You know what I mean," I firmly say. "Just yesterday, you were telling me we can only be friends, but today, I'm in *your* home, in *your* Jacuzzi, with *your* hands on me."

"Didn't you come out here in *that* because you were expecting something to happen?" he asks, his eyes dropping down to my cleavage.

"No!" I lie through my teeth, looking away from him.

"Don't look away from me, Takara," his tone is stern and has me looking back at him. "Good girl."

That praise, that little praise, sends my body into a fluttery mess. Why do I like it so much?

"Now then, why did you wear this?" he asks even though I'm pretty sure he knows I was lying.

"No reason." I shrug.

"No reason?" His eyes turn dark. "So, you just dress like this for anyone? Any male?"

"No!" I exclaim.

"Then tell me the truth," he demands.

"Fine!" I burst out with emotion. "You want to know why I wore this? Yes, it's because I had expectations."

He just stares at me. He's really going to make me say it, isn't he?

Taking a deep breath, I say, "I was hoping that tonight, you would fuck me."

Within a single moment, his mouth is on mine.

I moan at the feeling of his lips pressed against mine. It feels like forever since I've kissed him, and it really has been a long time. Three weeks.

I've missed this, this feeling. Kissing him is definitely nothing like kissing someone else. It's different. Better. On so many different levels.

His fingers grip my skin and my arms wrap around his neck. He pulls me flush against him, our skin sticking together like one as a result of the water. He's shirtless and my torso is bare, leaving nothing between us. His one hand travels down and I gasp when he touches me *there*. I'm soaking wet down there, and not just because of the water, and I know he knows it.

He groans when he feels how slick I am through my bikini bottoms.

"Take it off," I breathe into his mouth. "Please."

I'm aching to be released from my cotton binds. I want him to touch me there, with no material between us.

He tugs at the material, like wants to rip it off. I want him to. Then he pulls on the lace, until it tears and comes floating in the water. I moan when he touches me bare, his thumb flicking my clit. I break the kiss, my head going to his shoulder. I latch my lips onto his shoulder, muffling my moans as he caresses me, so gently and slowly, it drives me crazy.

Then he slides a single finger inside my heat, and I throw my head back. He trails kisses down my neck, suckling and biting on my sensitive skin. He starts moving his finger in and out, in and out, in and out. Curling it until it brushes against a spot inside me that has me seeing stars.

Moving my hand down, I reach into his boxer briefs and wrap my fingers around him. He groans in response, adding another finger into me. I start moving my hand up and down his shaft, his fingers moving insistently inside of me, and I move with him, chasing my release.

With a few more strokes, I come undone, crashing in his arms. He follows soon after me, groaning out loud as he finds his release.

He kisses me again, his lips insistent and passionate. I kiss him back, revelling in the feeling.

Then I get bolder, reaching down to push his underwear down his hips until he springs free, all hard and thick. Pushing myself against him, I lift myself a little so that my centre is positioned right above him.

"Wait," Avery breaks the kiss when he realises what I'm about to do. "Not like this."

My mood deflates.

"Do...do you not want to?" I hate how pitiful I sound.

"Of course, I want to, baby," he says, brushing a hair out of my face. "But I want to make our first time together special for you. Not some quickie in a hot tub. You deserve better than that."

I purse my lips, and then I nod.

"Please don't look like that, baby," he pleads. "I want to make this good for you."

I have no doubt he will.

Then I realise. I haven't told him I'm a virgin yet, and here I was, about to slide onto him without him even knowing.

"Now, shall we get out? Let me wash you," he says.

I can't help but smile.

"Someone seems to like washing me," I tease.

"I'm not going to even try and deny it," he confesses, and I laugh, before nodding.

"Okay," I agree, wrapping my legs around his waist. He groans.

"You're killing me here." He groans, but I just laugh. He gets out of the Jacuzzi with me in his arms and carries me inside. He carries me right to his bedroom and into the bathroom in there. I stare at the bathroom in awe. I don't think I'll ever get used to how fancy it is.

Avery chuckles at my reaction, squeezing my waist.

Instead of placing me in the bath like last time, he carries me into the large shower that could probably fit a whole family in it.

"You going to get down now?" he says more than asks and I pout but unwrap my legs from around him and let him lower me to my feet. Now, he towers over me. Literally.

"You owe me a new bikini," I tell him, staring down at my bare bottom.

"I'll buy you as many as you want," he promises.

Then he unclips the clasp of my bikini bra and lets my breasts spring free. He tosses the bra aside, leaving me completely naked in front of him. I feel the need to cover myself with my arms and hands, but he stops me.

"You're perfect," he says. "Just the way you are."

I blush, and the redness travels down my entire body. He smiles, tugging his underwear down his legs and tossing it aside carelessly. Now, we're both completely naked. I can't help but think of what we can do in here. The thought of having shower sex has my body flushing redder, if that's even possible.

But I doubt he'd allow it. At least not for our first time together.

I think it's really sweet of him for being so caring, but I wish he'd jump me already.

The thought makes me laugh.

"What's so funny?" he asks. I shake my head. "Come on. Tell me."

The little hint of a whine in his voice has me smiling.

"Let me wash you first." I change the subject, and although he pouts, he lets it go. I grab a loofah from the shelf and some soap, getting just enough soap on it before starting to wash him. I drag the loofah over every inch of him, surprise flashing in my eyes when I see that he is indeed hard again, standing long and proud against his abdomen. I secretly smile out of his vision before washing him there, causing his breath to hitch.

I love the effect I have on him.

"Bend down, please," I request, spreading shampoo all over my hands. He bends down, his face coming down eye level with my chest. The way he stares at my breasts, with so much wonder and desire has me clenching my thighs together. He notices but doesn't say anything.

I lather his hair with shampoo, massaging his scalp and making him hum in satisfaction. Then we swop, and he's washing me next, making sure to get into every crevice and nook of my body. Then when he gets to my legs, he pries them open with his hands, and almost immediately, my wetness drips onto the shower floor, trickling down my thighs.

I close my eyes in embarrassment, but he doesn't comment on it, just washing in between my legs quietly. Well, I guess he can't exactly tease me, especially when he's very much and obviously aroused himself.

When he's done with my body, he proceeds to wash my hair and I lean my forehead against his chest when he massages my scalp with his expert fingers. Its so relaxing, I nearly fall asleep.

"You tired, baby?" Cameron asks and I nod, humming. "Let's get out then."

He picks me up into his arms and carries me out of the shower. He sets me down on the marble counter just to dry himself and me off, and then I'm in his arms again and he's carrying me back into his bedroom.

"You want something to wear?" he asks me and I nod. As much as I want to sleep completely naked next to him, I don't want to take any risks of me possibly jumping him in his sleep.

He helps me into a plain white shirt that reaches just above my knees. I feel like such a baby right now. His baby. And I love it. He doesn't seem to mind taking care of me either, so that's a bonus.

He pulls on a pair of underwear and then joins me in bed. I immediately curl up against his side, and he wraps an arm around me. I hum in satisfaction.

"Sleep tight, my love." is the last thing I hear before drifting off to dreamland.

CHAPTER 20 – AVERY

She's so beautiful.

So perfect.

And all *mine*.

I know we haven't made it official yet, but in my mind, and in my heart, she's mine, and no one can take her from me.

Kara sleeps soundly in my arms, her fingers wrapped around my bicep tightly as she sleeps. I can't seem to wipe the silly smitten smile off my face, and I don't want to either.

Last night, this little baby wanted to have sex with me. I nearly came in my underpants when she said those words.

"I was hoping that tonight, you would fuck me."

I wanted to. I really wanted to. So badly. But this little baby can't just get fucked raw, not on the first go anyway. Because I knew, when I slid my fingers inside her, she's a virgin. She hasn't told me yet, and I'm not sure if she's ever going to, but it's okay, because I already know. I don't have much experience deflowering virgins. Hell, when I lost my virginity, the girl had already had sex before me. So, this is unchartered territory for me too. But I want to make it good for her. I know the first time hurts for a girl, so I want to make sure she's completely ready, not just mentally, but physically too.

Kara stirs in my arms, pulling me out of my thoughts. For a moment, I think she's awake, but then I hear soft snores, and I smile, unable to stop myself from placing a soft kiss on her head.

She's so precious. How did I ever get so lucky?

"Ave," she mumbles in her sleep. "Please touch me."

I twitch in my underpants. Is she...having a wet dream? About me?

Then she moans, bending her knee of the leg that's in between mine. I tense up when she brushes against me, and I instantly harden.

"Baby," I whisper. She needs to wake up now, or so help me God, I won't be able to control myself. "Baby, wake up."

She just groans in response. Knowing she's having a wet dream about me is a huge turn on in itself, and now she's touching me too? Oh Lord, have mercy on me today.

"Baby," I say, a little louder this time. But she doesn't wake up. Then I get an idea. I can't be the only one having a hard time this morning.

Trailing my hand under my shirt that she's wearing and cup her naked heat. She gasps in her sleep, her body arching into me. I start moving my hand up and down, flicking and pinching with my fingers every now and then.

"Ave," she moans, her eyes shut tightly closed. The little baby is awake. "It-it feels so good."

I move my hand faster and her body starts jerking in my hold. She starts moving with me, chasing her release. But just as she's about to come, she grabs my hand and stops my movements.

My eyebrows furrow in confusion.

"I-I don't want to stain your sheets," she stammers, her eyes finally fluttering open.

"You really think I care about that?" I ask her. She slowly shakes her head. "Then why?"

"I-I was having a wet dream, about you," she admits, covering her face with her hands. I smile. This innocent little baby.

"I know, baby," I tell her, prying her hands away from her face. "But there's no need for you to be embarrassed. Do you have any idea how many wet dreams I've had about you?"

"Really?" she squeaks out, her eyes becoming big. I nod.

"Every. Single. Night." I end off with a kiss to the base of her neck.

"Avery, do you mind morning breath?" she suddenly asks.

"No, why-"

She cuts me off with a kiss. Its quick and over before I can even kiss her back. I pout.

"That's not fair," I protest, trying to pull her back to me, but she ducks out of my hold, climbing out of bed.

"Maybe not, but I got to see you pout, so that's a bonus for me," she says, cheekily sticking her tongue out for me, and then she runs into the bathroom with a giggle. I don't know if she's hoping I'll follow her, but I do, and it turns out that she didn't lock the door. So she was hoping.

I run to her, wrapping her in my arms the moment I see her standing next to the toilet. She squeals.

"I have to pee, Avery!" she exclaims. Then I make a point to lift the toilet lid and place her on it. She looks at me expectantly, waiting for me to leave.

"So, go ahead. Pee," I say, laughing when her jaw drops.

"You are not watching me pee." She actually sounds horrified at the prospect.

"From this moment on, there's going to be no secrets between us," I simply tell her.

"How is me peeing alone me keeping a secret?" she snaps, glaring up at me. I merely chuckle. She's trying to look tough, but with that cute face of hers, she can't pull it off. At least not to me. "No way...You don't have a weird kind of fetish that has to do with watching your significant other peeing, do you?"

She cringes before I even answer.

"And if I do?" I challenge. She purses her lips.

"Well, usually that would be a dealbreaker, but it's *you* we're talking about, so, I guess I could learn to live with it," she says after much contemplation. I smile. I don't have a weird fetish like that, but it is nice to know she'd still be with me even if I did.

"I was kidding," I say with a chuckle and winking at her before walking out of the bathroom.

I wait on the bed for Kara. She takes quite a while, and I chuckle. She must be feeling shy now.

I decide on ordering in some breakfast because it's a Saturday and after working so hard all week, I feel like being lazy today. I think Kara would appreciate it too, especially after cooking up that feast for us last night. I feel like waiting for Kara before ordering, but she takes too long and so I just order a range of food items. There ought to be something she likes amongst those I picked. If not, I'll just break my rule of Saturday being a lazy day and go out and buy her something else.

When I'm done placing the order, Kara finally emerges out of the bathroom.

"Have a good pee?" I tease, unable to stop myself, and it's worth it, because I get to see her blush. "C'mere."

She reluctantly walks over to me and gasps when I suddenly pull her onto my lap, her legs on either side of my thighs as she straddles me. I place my hands on her waist. I still feel bad for not being able to give her an orgasm, but something tells me she won't let me continue what we were doing earlier.

"What?" she asks, her eyes avoiding mine. "Why are you looking at me like that?"

"Like what?" I ask. She sends me a disbelieving look, but I'm honestly confused. "How do I look at you?"

She doesn't answer, her eyes unable to meet mine. I squeeze her waist.

"Tell me, baby," I prompt her, flashing her a reassuring smile. "How do I look at you?"

"Like...like I'm your world. Like...like I'm your everything."

It hits me right in the chest. I do look at her like that, don't I? But its not on purpose. It just happens, because that's how I feel.

"That's because you are, my love," I say, reaching up to cup the side of her face in my hand. She automatically leans into my touch, making me smile. "I know we don't know each other that long or that well, but you've quickly burrowed a whole in my heart, a whole only you can fill. You make me feel things I've never felt before. After you left that day...I was broken. We had only known each other a week then, but you already meant so much to me. Kara, you *do* mean the world to me. You *are* my everything."

She blinks through tears.

"No, don't cry, baby." I murmur, wiping a fallen tear away. She shakes her head with a trembling smile.

"It's happy tears, Ave," she says, squeezing my hand that's on her face. "I'm just really so happy right now."

I can't tell her I love her, but I know that I'm on my way there.

And for now, this is perfect enough.

CHAPTER 21 – TAKARA

You are my world. You are my everything.

I still can't believe Avery said those words to me. Well, not those exact words, but is so much better and sincere words, it melted my heart instantly.

It made me realise something myself.

I'm falling in love with him. It might seem fast to others, but I don't care, because I want to stay true to my feelings at all times, and this is what I *truly* feel.

I'm falling in love with Avery Wilde.

"What has you up in the clouds this morning?" my mother asks me as I walk into the kitchen. I'm surprised she's speaking to me. Usually, she's in her own buzz in the morning and doesn't bother speaking a word to me until late afternoon when we both come home.

"What do you mean?" I ask, feigning innocence. If only she knew I was thinking about my professor, her co-worker, twelve years my senior, and how I'm falling hopelessly in love with him.

"I know that look," she says, narrowing her eyes at me. "I wore it so many times when I was young. There's a boy in your life."

Well, I wouldn't exactly call Avery a *boy*...

I try to deny it, but my smile gives me away.

"And? When am I meeting him?"

"Mom, don't be so hasty," I exclaim. "This is all new."

"Oh my. Your first relationship. Your first boyfriend," my mother says, clasping her hands together. "My little Takara is all grown up now, isn't she?"

"Mom," I call out, my face creasing in worry. "Are you okay?"

"Of course I am. Why would you think that I'm not?" she questions.

I bite my tongue.

It's not nice to tell her the truth. The truth that is how she never paid any attention to me or ever offered me any sort of affection growing up. She might as well not even be there, the only trace of her in my life being the bills that she paid for my tuition. Now she's acting like she truly cares about me, and like she's...proud of me? It's weird.

I don't like how uneasy it makes me.

"I'm going to school," I announce, not answering her question.

"I'm leaving now too," my mother informs me, taking a long sip of her coffee. "We can go together."

"It's really okay," I start to say but she waves me off as she grabs her bag.

"I have a car and we're going to the same place, so there is no more reason for you to take the bus."

Her logic makes sense, but the thought of being alone in the car with her every single day for an hour at the least makes me so uncomfortable, I wish it didn't.

I know it's bad, feeling uncomfortable around your own mother, but that's how I feel, and I don't think that's going to change any time soon.

"I also found someone," my mother suddenly announces as we start driving to campus. My head snaps to hers in surprise, but also, it all makes sense now. How did I not realise this before? She's only treating me this nicely because she's *happy*, and that's all because of a man.

I try not to let the sting of disappointment get to me.

"Who is he?" I ask instead.

"Well, he works at the college too," she starts off, and I nod. So, they're colleagues. If they are colleagues, it means that they see one another every day, and that makes me wonder how long this has been going on. "He's also a little younger."

Younger? My mother is dating a younger man?

Suddenly, I don't feel so bad for being with an older man, because essentially, it's the same thing.

"Are you going to introduce me to him?" I ask, even though I called her hasty for asking the same question earlier, but I have a reason for that. This is my first relationship and so me wanting to take things slow is understandable, whereas I've seen my mother go through man after man since my father passed on.

"Actually...you've already met him," my mother says. I what?

"Is he a professor?" I ask, and she nods. A professor at my college...a professor I know and have met before...who could it be?

I can count my college professors on my fingers, but there's still too many options for me to be able to deduct who it is exactly. I guess I'll have to wait until my mother formally introduces me to him.

"Anyway, I'm happy for you, mom," I say, smiling at her, and its true. Now that I'm so happy in my first romantic relationship, I want her to be happy too, and find that happiness somewhere besides a wine bottle.

"Thank you, Kara. I'll introduce you to him soon," she promises and I nod. My mother looks very excited by the prospect of introducing this new man in her life to me, her daughter, and something about the sparkle in her eyes tell me that its serious this time. No more flings like in the past. It must be serious this time.

The rest of the car ride is silent, but neither my mother nor I hide our happy smiles on our faces. Now I finally feel like I can be happy *freely*.

"Shall we go home together?" my mother asks when we arrive at the campus. I shake my head.

"I'm having a late lunch with Zoe after class, so I'll be home after that," I inform my mother who nods and waves me goodbye as I get out of the car. I walk straight to the history building, abruptly stopping halfway on the way there when I realise my history class isn't until later.

Pouting in disappointment, I text Zoe, asking her where she is. She tells me she has a class now and that I can join her if I don't have a class right now, which I reply to with a yes and start heading to that building instead.

Zoe is waiting outside the building when I arrive and she hooks her arm around mine before we walk to the lecture hall.

"Let's sit at the back. I don't feel like answering questions today," Zoe says and I nod before we take our seats in the last row in the corner of the auditorium. "So? No history this morning?"

I shake my head. "Later."

"You sound disappointed," Zoe tells me, eyeing me with suspicion. And then I realise. I haven't filled Zoe in on anything that's happened between Cameron and I. I was just so stuck in my own head and daydreams that I completely forgot. How could I though, when she's the one person who will support me no matter what I do?

"Zoe, I have something to tell you," I announce.

"What is it?" she asks.

"I'll tell you after class," I tell her, but she shakes her head.

"No, tell me now," she demands. "We're sitting at the back with no one close to us so we won't be eavesdropped upon. So? What is it?"

"You see...the thing is..." I trail off. She sends me a look that tells me to just come out and say it. "I'm seeing Avery!"

It comes out louder than I meant for it to, but luckily, the other students are too busy with their own things to pay attention to the two of us.

"Avery?" she repeats. I nod. "As in Avery Wilde? Your history professor Avery Wilde?"

I nod again. Then she squeals, startling me.

"You lucky duck. When did this all happen?"

Then I proceed to tell her everything, besides the intimate details of course, and include how Cameron formally asked me out. It was beautiful, that night. It was Saturday night and we were back in the hot tub, staring up at the night sky when he asked me to be his girlfriend. I was surprised, but didn't hesitate to jump into his arms, shouting yes. I probably could have done a better job at hiding how elated I was, but I didn't feel the need to. I don't want to hide anything from him.

When I'm done letting her in on everything, she squeals again. She looks just as excited as I was when he asked.

"But...there is something that's been bothering me a little. Just a little," I admit.

"What is it?" Zoe asks.

"What if...what if this is a mistake? We're basically forbidden lovers, and there's so much at stake, especially if we are found out. I was just worrying if it's all worth it in the end."

"Are you happy?" Zoe suddenly asks, and I immediately have an answer.

"Yes."

"Then the minor details such as your age gap and that doesn't matter. What matters is the now, and how this relationship makes you feel. As long as you're happy, it'll always be worth it."

Zoe is so wise sometimes, and not only because she has way more experience with men and relationships than me.

"Since we are speaking of him," Zoe starts off, leaning in closer to me. "Can I come with you to your class today?"

She sends me a hopeful smile.

"Of course," I easily agree. There's no reason for me to tell her no.

"Yes!" she silently cheers, making me laugh. Then I think of her relationship she's in right now.

"By the way, how are things going with you and Derek?" I ask.

"Good," she says. "We had sex on Friday night. And Saturday night."

"Was it your first time?"

"With him? Yes."

"And? How was it?"

I'm surprisingly more eager than I usually would be, but I have a feeling its because I'm at the point where I'm going to have sex soon too.

"It was...great."

I blink in confusion.

"Why do you sound like that?" I ask her.

"Look, its nothing bad. It's just...from an older guy like him, I thought he would be...you know...rough and throw me around and stuff," she confesses. "But he was gentle and trust me. There's nothing wrong with that. It's just...I was hoping at some point, when we were used to one another like *that*, he would get bolder, and more...adventurous."

"But it was just..."

"Vanilla," she ends the sentence for me.

I lean back in my seat, pondering on her words.

"What do you think? Do you think I'm just overreacting?" she asks me. "Do you think I expected too much from him?"

"It's not your fault, Zoe," I tell her. "When we think of older men, we do imagine them to be dominant and rough in bed as a sign of their experience. That's true. But you have to remember. While he's an older and more experienced guy to you, you're a younger and less experienced girl to him. So, he might hold back because he doesn't want to hurt you or push your boundaries. Which means that you need to be open with him about how you feel."

I'm surprised by all the words that just left my mouth. When did I get so wise when it comes to this stuff?

"And if nothing changes?" she asks.

"Is sex that important in a relationship?" I ask her instead.

"Of course there are other important factors, like your feelings for one another, but ultimately, yes. It might sound cruel, but most of the time, simply liking each other isn't enough. Because one day, you may marry this person, and signing up for unsatisfying and boring sex is not something I want."

"Is sex with him that boring?" I ask.

"Not yet," she defends. "But, if I'm being honest, I'm scared that one day, I will get bored of it."

Will get. Not might get but will get.

"Look, I know myself. I *will* get bored at some point, and then I might end up doing something I'll regret," she admits.

Wow. How did the class turn into this?

"For now, just talk to him. Then we'll see how things go," I advise her, and she nods. That's the end of that discussion.

While Zoe focuses on the lecture for the rest of the time, I just lean back in my seat and think about Avery and md. In my opinion, I think we are pretty compatible physically. Yes, we haven't gone all the way yet, but we've done some intimate things and got each other off, so that's a good sign. I think.

I hope.

CHAPTER 22 – TAKARA

I can't take my eyes off him.

And because we're in a lecture, I don't have to.

Avery looks so handsome today, in his black trousers and plain white shirt with the sleeves pulled up until his elbows, revealing his tattoos. That singular silver band on his index finger glints in the light, and his hair is messy like it always is. My favourite.

I smile, leaning my face on my hand.

I can't believe it. This man...is *mine*. All mine, and no one else's. How did I get so lucky, to find a man who treats me like a queen, who isn't shy in expressing his emotions, and who makes me feel so much, it's scary sometimes.

Then his eyes meet mine. I sit up straighter, my eyes lighting up. I smile at him, and something flashes in his eyes, but it's gone before I can decipher what it means. He looks away and continues teaching, and I'm not disappointed. I'm satisfied with just that.

"Wow, you are definitely smitten," Zoe says from beside me and I nod, my smile not going anywhere. "And you suck at hiding it."

My head snaps to hers.

"Is it that obvious?" I ask her and she nods.

"It's not a bad thing. Just maybe, tone it down a little while we're here."

I nod, straightening my back. I have plenty of time to stare at and admire Avery, and the thought of being with him makes this little sacrifice worth it.

I don't pay attention to what is being taught in the lecture, only snapping out of my trance when the lecture ends and everyone starts packing up. I quickly shove my things into my bag, telling Zoe, "You go on first. I have to talk to Ave-Professor Wilde about something."

I don't wait for her response before I walk away and head straight to Avery's desk. All the students leave quickly, probably rushing to get

125

to their next classes, and I'm grateful. Now I get some alone time with Avery.

"Ms. Smith. How can I help you?" he asks, an amused smile on his face. He called me Ms. Smith on purpose, for fun.

"I have a problem, Professor Wilde," I say, feigning distress. He leans forward in anticipation.

"What may be the problem?" he asks.

"Missing you too much," I break out into a smile and he laughs.

"Well, I can relate, because I have the same problem," he says. He stands up and rounds the desk to get to me. Then he leans down and places a soft kiss on my lips.

"Hey, you're taking chances here," I tell him, trying not to show him how much I liked it. That simple kiss.

"Life is all about taking chances, baby," he says, his voice husky. Then he kisses me again, longer and slower this time, and I don't pull away, my eyes instinctively fluttering closed.

We really are taking chances doing this *here* of all places, but there's a certain part of me that gets excited by it all. I'd never admit that to anyone though.

When he pulls away, he's smiling, looking down at me with a certain softness in his eyes.

"Don't look at me like that," I say, playfully shoving him, and of course, he doesn't even move an inch. "You'll make my shy."

"That is the reason why." he says, and I reach out to shove him again, but he grabs me, wrapping his fingers around my forearm.

"Sneaky."

He smiles wider, and then, realization flashes in his eyes.

"Oh, right. I'm having lunch with your mom today," he tells me. My eyebrows raise.

"Why would you?" I blurt out.

"Because we're colleagues and she invited me," he says. "*And* she's your mother, Kara. When we eventually tell people about us, I want her to like me, not just as a colleague, but as a son-in-law."

Son-in-law. He said that. He really said that, didn't he?

I can't help but smile, wrapping my arms around him.

"So, you want to go public with me, someday?" I ask, and he nods, staring at me as if though he can't believe I'm even asking him this question.

"Of course," he says, leaning down. "I care about you, Kara. You're not going to be my dirty little secret. I won't degrade you like that."

There it is. The butterflies.

I've never felt it before, but I know that it is indeed butterflies. All caused by him. Avery Wilde. My professor.

"By the way, is your mother going to her friends again this weekend?" he asks, the hope in his eyes very obvious.

"Not sure," I decide to tease him. "Why?"

"Well, I wanted to take you somewhere," he says.

"I'll find out if she's going," I say, and he nods.

"Now, you should get going. I have another class soon," he tells me and I pout in response, but he just smiles, pressing a soft kiss on my lips. "I'll see you later."

Begrudgingly, I nod before walking out of his class.

CHAPTER 23 – AVERY

I miss her so much.

And it doesn't help that I'm sitting opposite her mother, having lunch with her right now. I was surprised when Mrs. Smith invited me out to lunch, and although I'm not completely comfortable with her, I didn't see any way how I could have possibly say no, with her being Kara's mother and all.

"I'm so glad you said yes to lunch," Mrs. Smith speaks up, a wide smile on her face. "I'm hoping we can get to know one another, if you're open to that."

I quirk an eyebrow at her. Get to know one another? So we may be friends...?

"Sure," I say, although, I'm uneasy. Why now, all of a sudden? We've worked together for a few years now, and never once, did she ever approach me. So why now? Ever since that night she invited me into her home.

"So, tell me about yourself," she says, leaning her chin on her intertwined hands.

"Well...there's not much to say. I moved here a couple of years ago after completing my doctorate and started working at the university.

"What about family? Any lovers?"

Now I'm confused. Why the hell does she want to know about my lovers?

Skipping over that, I decide to tell her about my family, and *only* my family, "I have a sister, Chloe, but both our parents are deceased."

A frown creases her forehead.

"I'm sorry to hear that," she says, and she sounds truly sincere. I relax a little.

"It's okay," I assure her. "It's been a long time now."

She nods, and then she brightens up.

"Well, enough about the sad stories," she perks up. "Do you have a girlfriend?"

"Are you asking me because you want to set me up with someone or...?" I trail off with an awkward laugh.

"Oh! No! I'm just trying to get to know you," she tells me. "And I want to know *everything* about you."

Everything?

"So that we can be friends," she clarifies, and I release an uncontrollable breath of relief. Thank God. Where was my mind even going? She's Kara's mother for goodness sake. Why would I ever think she might want me?

"Yeah, we can do this," I say, although, I'm not comfortable enough with her to tell her about my dating life.

She smiles brightly, and then the waiter comes with our food.

The rest of the lunch is spent with her rambling on mindlessly, telling me things I didn't even ask for, but she seems to enjoy it. Talking about herself. This reminds me of what Kara said about her. She might be really self-centred after all.

But all in all, it wasn't so bad. I wouldn't consider it a waste of my time. If anything, this can work out. I can make her like me, and then hopefully, she won't react too badly to me dating her daughter.

*****

I stare up at the apartment building in the complex.

I've been standing here for the past half hour. After missing my baby like crazy, I drove mindlessly around town and somehow, I ended up here. At her apartment complex, and now like a complete creep, I've been staring up at her apartment for half an hour now.

I could call her, but for some reason, I feel nervous to. Maybe because I miss her like crazy, and I don't want to come off as obsessive. Although, I'm flirting with the line by simply being here right now.

Then my phone pings with a new message. I take it out of my pocket, my eyes lighting up when I see the name.

My baby <3: I miss you ☹

A smile spreads across my face. I'm not the only one.

Me: Come outside.

Within moments, her apartment front door bursts open and she comes running out onto the balcony. I laugh at her appearance. She's in her pyjama shorts and t-shirt and her hair is up in a messy bun, her feet clad in a pair of bunny slippers.

Her eyes scan all over, until they finally meet mine and I wave at her. A wide smile stretches across her face when she sees me and she turns before starting to run. I watch her run down the stairs, descending floor by floor, until she finally reaches the bottom and runs right to me, launching herself into my arms.

I laugh, hugging her tightly. It's not normal how much I've missed her, especially when I see her every day in class, but I don't care. Even though I see her in class every day and we chat and call every day, I still miss her. Because I don't get to touch her, hold her in my arms, or kiss her.

"What are you doing here?" she breathes out against my chest.

"I missed you too much," I admit, inhaling the smell of her apple scented shampoo. She pulls away slightly so that she can look at me. She stares at me for the longest time before I laugh. "What?"

"You seem to get more handsome every day," she says, and I laugh out loud.

"And you look absolutely ravishing," I say, eyeing her. It's now that she's so close to me that I notice that she isn't wearing a bra, the cold breeze causing her nipples to harden into small pebbles.

She blushes in response.

"If I knew you were coming, I'd have dressed better," she says, blushing in embarrassment.

"Really?" I ask, and she nods. "I think you look perfect right now though."

She presses her body into mine in response, the feeling of her nipples against me causing me to harden instantly. Fuck.

She doesn't seem to notice the effect she has on me though, unconsciously rubbing herself on me.

"Is your mom home?" I breathe out. She shakes her head. "Will she be home soon?" Another no. "Then let's go up."

She doesn't protest, letting me pull her up to her apartment. The moment we are inside and the door is closed behind us, I grab her and pull her into me, kissing her. She gasps in surprise. I press my hardness against her stomach, and she moans upon feeling my arousal.

I push her back until the back of her knees hit the edge of the couch. I let her fall down onto the couch, crawling over her. She's very eager tonight, her fingers already reaching up to unbutton my shirt. I pull it off me when it's all unbuttoned, and she sucks in a breath at my bare chest. She reaches up, running her fingers down my chest to my abs, stopping at the hem of my pants.

"Will you take it off?" she asks, her eyes pleading. I smile, leaning down before popping open the button of my pants.

"Only if you take off that t-shirt," I tell her. "I want to see those perky little nipples of yours."

She blushes but doesn't hesitate in pulling the t-shirt over her head, leaving her chest completely bare. And boy, is it a feast. I lean down, capturing one of her hard nipples in between my lips. She moans, her back arching off the couch. I swirl my tongue around her sensitive bud, lifting my hips to let her push my pants down my hips and thighs.

She tugs at my hair, pulling my head up to kiss me again. The kiss is wild, full of teeth and tongue. I've never been so desperate for a woman before, it's almost overwhelming.

"Take me to bed." she practically begs, and I pull away, scooping her up in my arms and carrying her to her bedroom. Laying her gently on the bed, I pull her pyjama bottoms down her legs along with her panties. Then I pull down my pants the rest of the way along with my own underwear and tossing it onto the floor.

I crawl over her, laying kisses all over her sensitive skin on my way to her lips. Then I'm overcome with the need to taste her. Fuck, I *need* to taste her. Now.

I crawl back down her bed, until my face is between her legs, and I can *smell* her.

"Ave," she whimpers, the embarrassment evident in her voice.

"Relax baby," I tell her. "Let me have a taste."

Instinctively, she spreads her legs for me. And then I go in for it. I practically devour her, lapping up all of her arousal with my tongue. I'm like an animal, feral, and I can't get enough of her.

She tastes so sweet, like a juicy little fruit, like something I've been craving all my life. Her loud moans fill the room and it just spurs me on. I suck on her clit, causing her toes to curl. Then I thrust my tongue into her wet heat, my tongue seeking, and within a few moments, she comes, so hard she squirts onto my tongue. I swallow all of her orgasm, some of it even dripping down my chin.

When I move back up to her, I kiss her, letting her taste herself on me. She moans, wrapping her arms around me.

"I want you," she says, the heels of her feet digging into my back. I want her too. It would be so easy. She's so wet, I bet I could just slide myself in with one thrust. But not yet. The timing isn't right just yet.

But I'm so hard. So *fucking* hard. I need a release.

So, I press myself against her, rubbing my length against her wet folds. She moans, trying to pull me in, but I grab her hips, stopping her. I rub myself against her, quite shamelessly chasing my own release. Within a few moments, she's coming again, and this is all I need to find my own release, my cum spurting out of me and onto her wet cunt, coating her completely in it, and I swear, I see some going inside her.

With a heavy breath, I collapse beside her, pulling her into my arms.

"Why didn't you –"

"Not tonight," I cut her off, knowing exactly what she was about to say.

"Then when?" she asks.

"Soon," I promise her. "Very soon."

Because I don't know how much longer I can control myself.

CHAPTER 24 – TAKARA

I wake up with a smile.

Ever since that night in my apartment with Avery, I've been on a constant high. Nothing can break me down now.

I get ready for college and join my mother for breakfast. We've fallen into a routine. Wake up, have breakfast, and then leave together. I'm still not completely comfortable with it, but I can see that she's trying, and that's all I've ever asked for from her.

However, this morning, she seems distracted, her eyes glued to her phone.

"Mom, are you okay?" I can't help myself but ask. She looks up, a smile on her face.

"Of course."

"Then what are you looking at?" I ask, taking a bite out of my toast. Then she flips her phone around and thrusts it in my face. At first, it's a little blurry from the abruptness of it all, but then when it's clear, my heart drops to my stomach.

It's a picture of my mother and...*Avery.*

They're both staring at the camera with smiles on their faces. Why is Avery in a picture with my mother? And why was my mother staring at this very picture like that?

"Mom...what is this?" I ask, anxiety wrapping around me like a blanket. Something is very wrong here.

"Well, you remember me telling you about my mystery man?" Mother says. No. Please no. "Well, its Professor Wilde."

I think I'm going to be sick.

My mother likes Professor Wilde. She likes Avery. *My* Avery.

Oh God.

CHAPTER 25 – AVERY

This is it.

The time is coming.

If Kara's mother leaves tonight, I'm going to take Kara with me, and if she doesn't, I'm still going to take her with me. We'll just say she's with that friend of hers.

I've planned everything. A romantic getaway to a little remote cabin by the lake. And then at the end of this weekend, I'm going to take her virginity. I'm ready. And I know she's definitely ready. So, it's going to happen this weekend.

I can't wait.

Then suddenly, my office door bursts open and Kara barges in.

"Baby –" I cut myself off when I see the tears running down her face. I'm up from my seat and by her side in an instant. "What's wrong? What happened?"

She buries her face in my chest.

"What happened, baby?" I ask, worried. She shakes her head.

"It's ruined," she cries out. "Everything is ruined."

"What's ruined?" I ask.

"Everything."

"What are you talking about, Kara?" I ask, pulling her back slightly so that I can look at her.

She's crying so hard; it tears my heart in two. I've never seen her like this before, and it scares me. A part of me wonders if maybe I did something wrong. But she wouldn't be here, holding me so tightly if I'm the cause. She's been so happy lately. What could have possibly happened now to change that?

"What's wrong, baby? Talk to me." I plead, but she shakes her head.

"I can't. It's all just...so much. Too much."

Then I realise. I know what to do.

"Okay, let's go," I say, packing up my things on my desk.

"Where are we going?" she asks.

"Somewhere far away," I tell her.

"Can we?" she sniffles. "Can we really?"

I turn to her, grabbing her hand.

"Of course we can," I tell her. For some reason, she needs reassurance, and if it makes her feel better, I'm willing to give it all to her. Over and over again.

She nods, looking thankful. I grab my things and her hand before leading her out of my office. Luckily, it's very early and so there are no students around to see us like this. Not that I care though. I'm not letting her hand go. Not now.

Not ever.

*****

We arrive at the cabin.

Kara has calmed down significantly since we left, although, she's still very quiet and unlike herself.

"Where are we?" she speaks for the first time since we left.

"I booked the cabin for us for the weekend," I inform her. "I was originally going to get you after class, but..."

She looks down.

"Anyway, we're here now, so let's just forget about everything and just be here, together, okay?"

She looks relieved at my suggestion, nodding thankfully. I still want to know what upset her so badly though, however, I'll back off for now. What she needs right now is not an interrogative boyfriend, but a caring boyfriend, and I'm going to be that for her. For as long as she needs me to be.

I lead her into the cabin. It's a nice little cabin, all rustic with everything being made of wood. There's a small little living room with a fireplace and a little kitchen at the end and a hallway on the side that leads to the bedroom and bathroom. I chose a cabin with only one bedroom for a reason.

"Can I go lay down?" Kara asks. I nod, watching as she disappears down the hall with a sigh. I spend the rest of the morning in the living room watching TV, however, I can barely focus on what I'm watching because my mind is stuck on Kara. I'm worried about her. I've never seen her like this before, and its honestly so scary. I don't even know what to do to make her feel better, especially since I don't even know what upset her.

But then suddenly, Kara appears by my side and she crawls onto my lap, wrapping her arms around my neck.

Placing my hands on her waist, I ask her, "Are you feeling better now?"

She nods, much to my relief.

"I guess the nap helped," I say, and she nods, although, there's a determined look on her face that wasn't there before. "You look determined."

She nods.

"I've decided," she announces. "I'm not going to let this get me down. At least for this weekend, I want to be selfish, and take what *I* want."

"Selfish about what?" I can't help but ask, my curiosity getting the better of me.

"You."

"Me?"

"Yes. You," she repeats. "You're all that I want."

I blush. Fuck, I blush.

She smiles at me blushing, but I look away, suddenly becoming shy. Why the hell am I becoming shy? I'm never shy.

"You're cute," she murmurs, leaning forward. "So. Fucking. Cute."

Then she kisses me, surprising me. She pulls away before I can respond, and I pout in disappointment.

"Avery." she calls out softly.

"Yes, baby?" I hum.

"I love you."

I freeze, my eyes widening.

Did I hear her right?

She...loves me?

"You don't have to say it back," she assures me. "I just wanted you to know that."

I love her. I do love her too. But...the words won't come out.

Why can't I say them? Its easy right. It's just three little words. So why the hell is it so hard for me to say?

"I...I care for you," I say, cringing at the disappointment that flashes in her eyes. Then she nods, forcing a smile onto her face. She's upset. She said I didn't have to say it, but of course, she still wants to hear it. Who doesn't?

"What's for lunch?" she changes the subject, climbing off my lap, disappointment now filling me.

"There's a little town not too far from here. We can go buy some groceries," I suggest and she nods.

We head out to town. There isn't much to choose from, but there is one supermarket where we manage to find the essentials such as bread and milk.

"Can I have cereal for lunch?" Kara asks, her eyes lighting up at the though.

"Of course you can," I say with a laugh. She finds a cinnamon flavoured cereal and adds it to the cart with an excited dance. I smile.

I'm glad she's feeling better now. I hated it when she was upset.

When we're done, we return to the cabin.

I make myself a sandwich while Kara makes herself some cereal, humming in satisfaction when she has her first spoonful.

"I'm really glad you brought me here," she suddenly speaks up. "I really needed this."

"I'm glad you're feeling better now." I tell her, reaching out to place my hand on top of hers.

"Tell me Avery," she starts off, her eyes suddenly flashing with mischief. "What was the objective of the weekend?"

The lust in her eyes makes me hard immediately. Fuck, not yet Cameron. You promised you'd wait till the end of the weekend. You need to woo her first.

So, I shake my head.

"Not what you're thinking," I say, watching her face fall. "At least not for tonight."

Her face lights up again, and I can't help but laugh.

This girl is so eager to be with me.

She's going to end up killing me. I swear.

CHAPTER 26 – TAKARA

Avery and I lay in bed, in each other's arms.

We've both stripped down to our underwear, and it's a relief to feel his bare skin against mine. I haven't felt him like this since that night.

I'm trying not to think about my mother and what she revealed to me this morning, especially since I've decided to say screw. I'm going to be with Cameron no matter what, even if it's just for this weekend. But it still plagues my mind, and I'm having trouble hiding it from Cameron.

My mother is in love with him. That's what she told me this morning. He's the man she's been lusting after, wanting, for ages, and he just happens to be the same man that I love too.

I told Avery I love him, and his response was...disappointing to say the least. I didn't want to force him, but telling someone you care of them after they told you they love you...that's really heartbreaking. I know he didn't mean it like that, but I can't help but think. Does he really not love me? I thought he did. And that only made the disappointment even heavier to take.

I look up at him, but he's not looking at me. Instead, he's staring off into space, his eyebrows furrowed.

"What are you thinking about?" I ask him, touching my hand to his face. His eyes meet mine, serious and determined.

"I want to go public," he suddenly announces. My eyes widen in shock.

"So suddenly?"

"It's not sudden. I've been thinking about it for a while," he admits.

"But...but there's so many risks involved. You could lose your job," I point out.

"I know, but I've thought about this. *Really* thought about this, and I've come to a decision. I want to go public. I want everyone to know you're mine and that I'm yours. I don't want to be in the closet anymore."

"Ave..." I trail off, overcome by so much emotion. He pulls me closer, his eyes tender.

"I'm willing to give up everything, just if I can be with you," he says. Tears fill my eyes.

"I love you," I tell him, not waiting for a response before pressing my lips to his. He responds immediately, cupping my cheek in his hand. He pours his heart out in the kiss, and immediately, I know.

He loves me.

He doesn't say it, but he doesn't have to. Because he tells it to me in the way he kisses me, and that's enough. That's more than enough.

When he pulls away, my eyes are glistening.

"I-I-"

"I know," I cut him off. "I know."

"It's just...I have a hard time saying it," he starts off.

"I know," I cut in, but he seems to want to continue. He wants to tell me his story.

"I've never been in love before. At least not seriously. No one's ever made me feel this way before. No one's ever made me want to say those words. But you...you make me feel so much, its honestly scary. It's overwhelming."

"It is for me too," I admit. "But I'm embracing it. Because this...what we're feeling...its something positive. Something good. And it's a good scary."

"I just don't want to lose you, baby," he breathes out.

Immediately, I think of my mother. Would he still feel the same if maybe...he knew she was in the picture too?

"Avery, what do you think of my mother?" I can't help but ask, biting my lower lip in nervousness.

"Your mother?" he repeats in confusion. "I don't think much of her. She's your mother. That's it."

I nod.

"Why are you asking me this though?" he asks, suspicion lacing his tone.

"No reason," I shrug. "You're right. She's my mother, so I would like you to tolerate her."

I don't want to say like. I won't. I don't want him liking her. Not as my mother or as a lover.

"I'll admit. I don't like the way she's been to you in the past. But she's still your mother, and so for you, yes. I will *tolerate* her."

Nodding, I snuggle deeper into his touch.

That's all I needed to hear.

CHAPTER 27 – TAKARA

I know what's coming.

Or, at least, I'm hoping its coming.

Its eight in the morning when I leave the cabin. Luckily, Avery is a late sleeper and a deep sleeper because he barely felt me leave the bed. I put the pillow in his arms though, just in case.

I walk down to the little town nearby in search of only one shop, and surprisingly, I find it. Its ironic that there's only one supermarket here but they have a whole shop for *this*.

The moment I walk into the shop, my cheeks warm up when my eyes land on all the sets f underwear and lingerie. A shop assistant is at my side immediately, a polite smile on her face, her eyes void of any judgement. I'm glad, because obviously, I'm still young and probably have no place here and no place having a sex life.

"How may I help you?" she asks.

"Uh...I'm looking for..." What am I looking for, exactly?

"Is it your first time?" she asks. First time at a shop like this or first time having sex?

Either way, I nod, because yes to both. She hums in understanding before gesturing me to follow her.

"We have a selection of items for people just like you," she tells me, and although she could be implying some judgement, her tone of voice tells me otherwise. She's really just trying to help. "These pieces are not as revealing and leaves much to the imagination."

Leaves much to the imagination? Does that still matter if he's already seen me completely naked?

"So, is there a colour you like?" she asks.

"Red." I immediately say, remembering the way he looked at me when I wore that red bikini I wore to the Jacuzzi. She smiles, before grabbing a few red items that she sees.

"Try these on and see if you like any of them. If you don't, we can always look for some more options." she says, leading me to the fitting room. I try on a few pieces, but none of them appeal to me, and I'm about to give up when I fit on the last one.

Wow, is all I think as I stare at myself in the mirror.

It's simple, for the most part, however, there are two holes where my nipples are and another hole where my mound is. It's perfect for a man who likes to fuck his woman while she's still dressed. Is Avery such a man though?

I feel sexy though. I look sexy.

I want this one, I decide.

Stripping out of it and putting on my normal clothes again, I walk out of the fitting room with a determined look on my face, clutching the lingerie I've chosen to my chest. The shop assistant smiles when she sees me.

"I take it you've made a choice?" she says, and I nod. She takes the other ones from me and starts hanging them back up. "You can go pay in front."

I nod, but pause, turning back to her.

"Thank you," I tell her. Thank you for helping me. Thank you for listening to me and my choices. Thank you for not judging me.

She merely nods with a knowing look in her eyes. I go to pay and when I walk out of the shop, I feel embarrassed all over again. All these people, seeing me walk out of this shop...

I'm quick to leave the town, relief washing over me when the cabin comes into view. I hope Avery isn't awake yet because I need to hide this without him seeing. It needs to be a surprise.

To my luck, I find him still in bed, soft snores escaping his lips. I smile, finding the way he clutches the pillow to his chest incredibly cute. I hide the bag in the far corner of the closet before stripping back down to my underwear and climbing back into bed with him.

He sleeps for a while longer before he finally groans, reaching up to stretch out his limbs. When his eyes open and meet mine, he automatically smiles, but that transforms into a frown when he sees that he's cuddling a pillow instead of me.

"Why are you so far away?" he asks with a frown, grabbing the pillow and throwing it onto the floor. I giggle when he pulls me back into his arms. "I hate you not being in my arms."

"Then you should notice when it's a pillow and not me," I decide to tease him.

"I can't believe I didn't..." he mutters, sounding angry at himself. "I'm sorry baby. I won't let you go next time."

I nod, laying my head on his chest.

"I know you won't." I say. He places a soft kiss on my head, tightening his arms around me.

We lay in bed for another hour before my stomach rumbles and Cameron bursts out laughing while I pout in embarrassment. He carries me out of bed and to the kitchen, placing me on the kitchen counter before starting to gather ingredients for breakfast.

"What's for breakfast?" I ask, trying to peek over his shoulder but he's just so freaking tall.

"It's a surprise," is all he says. I spend the next half hour staring at his back because he won't let me see, although, I'm not complaining. Its quite the view, the sight of his back flexing and his muscles contracting with each movement he makes.

By the time he's done, there's a mouthwatering aroma in the air and my stomach rumbles once more in anticipation. When he's done placing everything on the table, my eyes widen at the feast he's made.

There's so much to look at. Lemon blueberry scones. French toast with syrup and strawberries. Belgian Foster Belgian waffles. Egg muffins. Tomato, basil, and caramelised onion quiches. There's even cake! A banana-nut waffle cake.

My mouth waters and without another thought, I dig in, starting simple with French toast. For most of the breakfast, Cameron just stares at me in awe at how much I can eat until I practically force feed him some food. When I'm done eating, I'm so full I think my stomach might burst.

"I'm taking you out tonight," Cameron announces.

"Where?" I perk up. There isn't much around here and the restaurants that are in the town are mediocre at best.

"It's a surprise." He uses the same words as before. I purse my lips to prevent myself from huffing. I'll just have to trust him again.

We spend the rest of the day resting, lying on the couch and watching TV. I somehow managed to talk Avery into having a Barbie movie marathon with me and we ended up watching every single Barbie movie on Netflix by the time it was late afternoon.

"Come on. Go get dressed." Cameron says, patting my leg. I groan, rolling off him.

"Can't we just stay here? Let's get some pizza and relax."

"We've relaxed all day," he points out. "Come on. I really have something special planned."

The little whine in his voice has me jumping up.

"Wear the dress on the bed!" he yells out after me. I walk into the bedroom and my eyes land on the dress lying on the bed. Its red – I roll my eyes at the irony – and really short with a slit that will probably go all the way up my thigh. My entire cleavage and legs will be on show, but it's just for him, so I don't care.

I put on the dress, dragging a brush through my hair and leaving it loose in its natural waves. I put on some lipstick and mascara before standing in front of the mirror. Right now, I don't look like the nineteen-year-old girl I am. I look mature. Like a woman.

Smiling in satisfaction, I leave the bathroom and look for Cameron in the living room, but he's not there. Frowning, I'm about to call him when I see a little piece of paper of the table.

Meet me at the lake behind the cabin.

Love, Avery

Smiling, I drop the note and rush to the back of the cabin where the lake is. The moment I'm there, my breath is stolen away. Avery prepared a whole romantic dinner with candles lighting the darkness of the night. It must be fate, but the stars shimmer right above our table, making everything look extremely romantic, and then to add to all of it, there's lanterns floating in the lake water. Literal lanterns!

When did he plan all of this?

He's still busy setting the table when I run to him, my body collapsing against his back and I wrap my arms around him, resting my cheek on his back.

He's startled, but he's quick to place his hands over mine, squeezing.

Then he slowly turns around, my arms not leaving his body. His breath hitches when he looks at me.

"You look...wow," he breathes out, blinking. I smile, satisfied. I'm glad he likes it. He looks dashing himself, in a pair of black trousers and a crisp white shirt that he's pulled up at his forearms.

"You too," I chuckle. "Wow."

He laughs, grabbing my hand and turning around so that we are both looking at the view.

"Do you like it?" he asks, the nervousness in his voice tugging at my heart strings.

"Like it?" I scoff. "I love it!"

He breaks out into a broad smile.

"It's perfect, Avery," I tell him, and I'm being honest. "How did you even think to do all of this? How did you even plan this without me knowing?"

"Why do you think I never let you near the lake?" he retorts, and I laugh.

"I love it," I tell him, smiling. "So, what's for dinner?"

I gasp in awe when I see the food he's put on the table. Chicken and mushroom penne pasta with garlic bread. My favourite.

If it wouldn't end up with us not even having this date and heading to the bedroom instead, I'd kiss him right now.

He pulls the chair to the back for me, like a gentleman, before sitting opposite me.

"Appletizer?" he asks, holding the bottle up and I laugh with a nod. One would think there'd be wine at a date like this, but he knows my alcohol tolerance is low and I can't afford to get drunk tonight. It will ruin everything.

He pours me and himself the drink. I stare at the food.

"Wow, it looks so nice, I don't even want to eat it," I say.

"Well, it's not a feast for the eyes so you'd better eat," he tells me.

Smiling, I take my first bite. I moan in delight, the flavours bursting on my tongue.

"This is bad," I say, his brow raising in questioning. "You are a much better cook than me. What will I bring to this relationship?"

He bursts out laughing at me genuine question.

"*You* are enough," he says, his eyes filled with sincerity. "Just you."

I lean over, grabbing his hand.

"Wait, let's eat before we both get emotional," I say with a chuckle, laughing off the tear that escaped my eye. He wipes it away with his thumb before nodding and we continue eating.

I end off my dinner with my third piece of garlic bread, and its only now that I realise eating so much of it was probably not the best idea, because now I have garlic breath. I'll have to brush my teeth when we get inside.

"I'd invite you to go swimming, but with the lanterns, it's a little dangerous," he says, pointing to them with a chuckle.

"Tomorrow," I tell him. "Tomorrow, I will skinny dip with you."

His eyes flash with desire and I feel it all the way between my legs.

This is it. It's happening. What I've been waiting for for so long, it's finally happening.

We both stand up together, our bodies gravitating towards one another. His one hand grabs mine, pulling me into him whilst his other hand threads through my hair. He tilts my head up, pressing his lips to mine. I moan, opening my mouth for him. Our tongues meet, tangling together in a way that makes me toes curl in my slippers. Yes, I wore slippers to the date because I wanted to be comfortable, but also because I didn't bring any heels since I wasn't expecting this. He didn't seem to mind though.

But then I remember what I bought this morning and I break the kiss.

"I have a surprise for you," I breathe out. "Meet me in the bedroom in five?"

He nods, desire swirling in his eyes, but he lets me go. I grab the bag that I so expertly hid in the closet before walking to the bathroom. When the lingerie is on my body, I suddenly feel self-conscious. I've been naked in front of him before, but somehow, this feels so much more exposing. Thank God I shaved.

I wrap a robe around my body before walking back to the bedroom, Cameron already sitting on the bed, waiting for me when I arrive. When he sees me in the robe, his eyes darken. I have a feeling he knows exactly what the surprise is.

"So, what's the surprise?" he asks through hooded lids. I walk over to him, climbing onto his lap, letting my legs straddle his thighs. I gasp when I feel how hard he is, how ready he is for me, and all we did was kiss. I'm glad, because I can feel how wet I am too, all from just one kiss. Well, that, and the anticipation of what is about to go down.

He grabs my hips, pressing himself against me. I should feel embarrassed when a patch of wetness appears on his crotch from my own arousal since there is nothing covering my mound underneath this robe, bur I'm not. No, I want him to know *exactly* how turned on I am. All for him.

He growls when he sees the wet patch, reaching down to touch me, but I grab his hand, stopping him before climbing off him and coming to stand right in front of him. His eyes are filled with anticipation as he stares at me, his fingers twitching like he's dying to touch me.

I grab the tie of the robe, teasing him by pulling it down slightly, revealing the swell of my breasts, flashing him red lace. His eyes widen, and he licks his lips. I smile, tugging at the tie.

And then the robe drops to my feet.

CHAPTER 28 – TAKARA

The robe pools at my feet.

The way Avery looks at me, eyes dark and hungry, makes me wet instantly. I approach him and straddle his hips.

"What is all this?" he asks, trailing his fingers across my waist.

"You've been going on about how you want to make our first time special for me, and so I wanted to do the same for you," I tell him. "Do you like it?"

"Like it?" he exclaims, tugging me forward by my hair. "I love it."

Then he kisses me, devouring me thoroughly.

"I'm going to make you feel *so* good, baby," he promises, and I grin, kissing him deeper. That's when he stands up with me in his arms and twists us around and lays me down on the bed, my head sinking into the plush pillow.

He cups my face in his hands, saying, "You're so beautiful."

Kiss.

"So cute."

Kiss.

"So kind."

Kiss.

"So perfect."

I giggle.

"So pretty."

I stare up at him with a soft smile, the sincerity in his voice and eyes tugging at my heartstrings.

"I love you, Avery Wilde," I tell him, placing a soft kiss to his lips. "Never forget that."

He smiles before kissing me again.

When he starts caressing my exposed skin, I whine.

"Don't go slow tonight, Avery," I tell him, watching as his brows push together, "I'm all prepped, don't worry. Now, please. Just get inside me."

He wastes no time in ridding himself from his pants and thrusting into my pulsing hole, my back arching off the bed as I moan. It still burns even though he's fingered me so many times already, but that's to be expected since it's my first time ever.

"You okay?" he asks in concern. I nod, unconsciously clenching around him, eliciting a moan from him.

"Fuck," he curses, his eyes screwing shut.

Then they suddenly snap open again, dark and wild.

"I'm going to fuck you now," he says, but it's more a warning than anything else and doesn't give me a chance to even respond before he pulls out completely, however, just as I want to whine in protest, he slams back inside me.

This continues on for what feels like hours, him taking me to the edge but then teasing me by pulling out until only his tip is inside me.

"Avery!" I whine and he grins wickedly. He really loves edging me.

That's when he decides to put me out of my misery and starts thrusting consistently again, snapping his hips until he hits a certain spot inside me that has me seeing stars.

"Avery!"

I come, so hard I feel my consciousness leaving me for a few seconds. I'm only brought back to reality when he comes too, a warm flood drenching my insides with his release.

He collapses on top of me, breathing heavily. I wrap my arms around him, holding him to me as we both come down from our highs. When he tries to pull back, I tighten my hold on him, instinctively clenching around his length that's still buried deep inside me.

"Kara," he moans. I smile. That's right. That's my name. It's my name he's moaning, and mine only.

Only mine from now on.

No one else's.

CHAPTER 29 – TAKARA

The first thing I see when waking up is Avery's smiling face.

I can't help but smile too, especially when he places a soft kiss on my forehead.

"Good morning, sleepyhead," he greets, and I roll over, placing my hand on his chest.

"Good morning indeed," I say, and he chuckles.

"How are you feeling?" he asks, brushing his fingers through my messy hair.

"A little sore, but totally up for doing it again," I say in a cheeky voice. He laughs, rolling on top of me.

"Oh, I've created a sex-craved monster. How will I ever keep up with you?" he dramatically says. He's teasing me, but I know he enjoys just as much as I do.

And then I remember.

"I promised you we would go skinny dipping today." I remind him.

"So?" he asks, frowning at the prospect of morning sex going out the window.

"*So*, there's no one around," I tell him, looking pointedly at him. His eyes light up.

"You want to get freaky in the lake?" he questions, and I smile, pushing him off me. I get up from the bed.

"Last one there is a rotten egg," I childishly say before running out the door. He's quick to catch me though, lifting me up into his arms, causing me to squeal in surprise.

"You can't beat me," he says, his tone quite cocky. Smiling, he carries me out to the lake. I expect him to put me down, but instead, he goes caterwauling into the water with me in his arms, water engulfing us completely.

When he swims up to the surface, I gasp for air.

"I wasn't expecting that, you jerk," I say, slapping his chest.

"That's what makes it fun," he says, his eyes twinkling with mischief.

Smiling, I wrap my legs around his waist, pressing my pelvis against his. He gasps in surprise and I smile victoriously.

"Oh, someone wants to get fucked," he says, his eyes darkening.

I lean forward, whispering into his ear, "*Hard*."

And then he's inside me, causing me to gasp in surprise. He starts fucking me, moving his hips up and down whilst still keeping the both of us afloat in the water. Impressive.

I press my lips to his, kissing him ferociously as he starts thrusting harder, snapping his hips in a way that has him hitting that most pleasure-filled spot inside me continuously.

I heard most women can't come from penetration alone, but with the way he's moving inside me, and with the speed that he's moving, I can already feel myself getting close to the edge.

"Don't stop," I beg. "Please."

"No fucking way," he promises, his thrusts becoming even faster, and within a few moments, I'm coming. Hard. I moan, throwing my head back. He reaches up with his one hand to grab my breast, squeezing mu flesh in between his fingers. "I absolutely *adore* your tits."

I feel my entire body flushing with heat, even in the cold lake water.

I've never liked my breasts before. They were always too *big*. But suddenly, I love them. Because he loves them. And I want him to love every single part of me.

Between him fondling my breast and the other hand stimulating my clit, I feel myself coming again, and this time, I am a bit embarrassed at how quickly that orgasm came.

"So fucking sexy," he says into my ear, and all my embarrassment washes away. And then he joins me, filling me with his cum to the point where I feel so full. He doesn't pull out immediately. It's something we've both come to do and enjoy. Him staying inside me even after orgasming. I hug him to me, my arms around his neck.

Suddenly, reality comes rushing back to me. This is our last day here at the cabin. We have to leave later, and then I have to go home, to my *mother*. How will I be able to face her, knowing that I just slept with the man she's in love with?

I feel terrible. How can I not? Even though she's not been the best person to me, she's still my mother, and despite everything, I love her.

"What's wrong, baby?" Avery asks, sensing the sudden change in me.

My mother is in love with you. That's the problem.

I should tell him. He deserves to know. But it's so hard. I don't want him to know, because I don't want to make him think twice about us. I'm so selfish.

"Just...just hold me. Please," I beg him, and he hugs me tighter in response.

This weekend, it was our time. My chance to be selfish. But after this, he wants to go public. Can I really do that? Can I really walk around and call him mine after my mother told me how she feels about him? Can I do that without being consumed by guilt?

Can I really make things work between Avery and me?

CHAPTER 30 – AVERY

Something is very wrong with my baby.

And she won't tell me what. She just tells me to hold her, to not let her go. I don't mind. I love touching her and holding her, but she's upset. Something is bothering her, and it kills me that she won't tell me what. I need to know in order to know how to help her properly.

We had the best weekend ever, and it was when we had to go home that everything became ten times worse. She looked down, no, not just down. She looked downright miserable. And I had no idea how to turn that frown upside down.

Now, its Monday, and back to work. Now that its classes, I can't even be alone with her anymore. So I can't ask her what's wrong one more time.

I walk into the history building with a frown. I hate not being able to help her.

"Congratulations, professor!" a student of mine exclaims, holding a thumbs up to me.

"Congratulations? About what?" I question with furrowed brows.

"About you dating," he says, and my eyes widen. Did people already find out about Kara and me? How? "I heard you're in a relationship with the admin lady."

I blink. Once. Twice. What?

"The admin lady?" I repeat, and he nods.

"Mrs. Smith I think is her name. I don't really know the admin people," he says with a chuckle, but I'm horrified. Mrs. Smith. Kara's mother. Everyone thinks I'm seeing her. But why? Why would anyone think that?

"Where-where did you hear this?" I ask him.

"It's just a rumour going around campus," he tells me. Suddenly, the pieces come together in my head. Kara being so upset and sad, it's because of this. I'm not sure how, but it has to do with this.

"Excuse me. I have to go somewhere," I say, turning on my heels and heading right for the admin building.

"Here to see your girlfriend?" the woman at front teases when she sees me walk in. Horror fills me once more. Does literally everyone know about this?

I'm about to tell her to call Mrs. Smith, but as if on cue, she comes walking in from down the hallway. Her eyes flash with surprise when she sees me.

"Professor Wilde," she speaks out, glancing nervously at the other woman who is staring intently at the two of us. "What brings you here?"

"We need to talk," I tell her, my voice stern. Her eyes widen.

"What about?" she asks, her voice innocent.

I glance at the other woman for a quick moment before bringing my attention back to Mrs. Smith.

"I assume you've heard the rumour."

"About the two of us?" she asks, and I nod. "Of course."

"And you haven't felt the need to correct anyone?" I ask her, baffled when she shakes her head.

"Look Professor Wilde, no, *Avery*. It's no secret how I feel about you."

What?

"And so when the rumour came up, I didn't correct it in hopes that you would realise your feelings for me too."

She looks so hopeful it makes me feel sick.

"What the fuck are you talking about?" I snap, causing her to flinch at my harshness. Even the other woman's eyes widen at my tone, as if she cannot believe what is happening before her. I should probably have asked to talk in private, but now I can't hold it in anymore. I'm just so angry.

"Avery –" she starts off, but I cut in.

"*Professor Wilde*," I growl. "I'm Professor Wilde to you."

Sadness flashes in her eyes, but she quickly composes herself.

"Professor Wilde. I'm in love with you," she suddenly confesses. "I have been for a while now, and I finally built up the courage to ask you out to lunch the other day."

What. The. Fuck.

"You can't be serious."

"I am," she says. "I'm in love with you, and I knew since the night you had drinks at my place, you felt the same way."

I was only there for Kara!

I close my eyes shut, taking a deep breath to calm myself down before looking at her again.

"I love someone else." I decide to tell her. Her eyes widen.

"W-what?" she stammers.

"It's true," I confirm. "I love someone, but it's not you."

She starts crying. She literally starts crying, and I cringe at the ugly fat tears that runs down her face. I feel awkward. I should probably comfort her considering the fact that I made her cry, but I don't want to. Not when I know how she feels about me.

And then I think.

"Does Kara perhaps know about your feelings for me?" I ask, softening my tone.

Her head snaps up to mine, her eyes red.

"What does that matter?" she snaps.

So she does know, and that's why she was acting that way at the beginning of our trip and then again at the end of her trip. Now I know why coming home made her so miserable. How could I have been so oblivious? So blind?

I need to find her. Now.

I make a move to leave, but Mrs. Smith wraps her fingers around my wrist, stopping me.

"Please," she begs. "Can't you just...look at me? For once?"

I feel bad for her. Rejection sucks.

And so, I do *look* at her. She was definitely beautiful in her prime, I can tell that. She's also really skinny despite having given birth to a child which is impressive. But she doesn't have those big breasts, those thick thighs, those wide hips that I love.

She's not the one that I love.

I need to tell my baby how I feel about her. Now.

So, I shake my head at Mrs. Smith, and thankfully, she lets go of me. I rush out of the admin building, dialling Kara's number on my phone. But no answer. I call her at least three more times, but still no answer. She's ignoring me on purpose, no doubt.

Fuck, how did things get so complicated, so fast?

I search all over campus for her, but I can't find her anyway. Cursing under my breath, I call her one more time. Finally, she answers.

"Kara," I breathe out.

"*Avery*," she cries out. Damn, that hurts.

"I know, baby," I tell her, trying to soothe her with my voice, but it doesn't work. I'm too far away. "Where are you?"

She just sniffles.

"Tell me where you are right now, Takara," I demand, using her full name so that she knows I'm dead serious.

"*L-library*." she sniffles.

"Stay there, baby," I tell her. "I'm coming."

I head straight to the campus library. I look all over the library for her and I'm about to call her again when I spot a small body, curled up into a ball, all hidden in the corner of the 2nd floor of the library.

"Kara?" I call out, unsure if it's really her, and when the person lifts their head, I swear I can hear my heart crack into two. "Baby..."

I rush over to her, kneeling in front of her and pulling her into my arms. She cries into my shoulder, her tears soaking my shirt, but I couldn't care less. She's *crying*. Because of me.

"It's all ruined, Avery," she cries out. "Everything is ruined."

She's repeating the same words she said at first, when she barged into my office on Monday. I should have insisted that day, that she tell me what happened, but I didn't want to push her, not when she was in such a vulnerable state.

"I'm so sorry, Kara," is all I can say. I know it doesn't change things, and that it doesn't make things better, but it's all I can say.

She pulls away so that she can look at me, her eyes so red from all the crying. How long has she been sitting here and crying already?

"Why are you sorry?" she asks. "I-it's not your fault that my mom..."

She can't even bring herself to say the words out loud. Good, because I don't want to hear them.

"You know that I don't feel the same way, right?"

She doesn't answer, and my eyebrows furrow in confusion. Does she not know?

"But you should," she says, confusing me more. "She's older, closer to your age, and she's more mature. I'm just...I'm just a little girl still."

"Baby, that doesn't matter to me," I tell her, cupping her face in my hands. "You're the one I *love*. Not her. It'll never be her. It'll always only be you."

"You...you love me?" she speaks out so softly, and my heart clenches as I nod.

"I'm sorry it took me so long to say it," I say, but she shakes her head, wiping away her tears.

"I love you too."

Then she kisses me, pouring all her emotions into this one kiss. She tastes salty on my tongue, but I kiss her back, holding her face in my hands.

And then the sound of a shutter going off fills the air for a single second.

She pulls away from me, her wide eyes settling on a student standing at the end of the bookshelf with his phone in his hand, the camera directed at us.

"Oh no..." Kara whispers, about to stand up and probably beg that student to delete the photo and not tell anyone about what he just saw, but I grab her arm, stopping her. I meant what I said about going public about our relationship, and what better time than now. It'll surely kill all rumours about me and her mother going around campus.

The student runs away with wide eyes, and Kara turns back to me with a glare.

"Why did you stop me?" she snaps.

"I told you, Kara. I want us to go public," I remind her.

"Like this? When everyone thinks you're dating my mother?" she exclaims in disbelief.

"Yes," I insist. "In fact, I think this is the perfect time."

And we didn't even have to come out of the closet ourselves. We were caught, as simple as that. I believe this was fate, and so I'm letting it run its course.

Kara sighs, slumping in my arms.

"What do we do now?" she speaks.

"Now, we wait."

CHAPTER 31 – AVERY

It didn't take long before everyone knew about Kara and me.

The picture of the two of us kissing was plastered all over the school gossip site. Some people were actually posting supportive comments, saying that love is love despite age while others find it disgusting and accuses me of grooming her, even though she's perfectly of legal age already.

I tried to hide all the bad comments from Kara, because I know how she will react. Before even thinking about defending herself, she'd try to defend me, and I don't want to put her in that position. I've done enough.

Her friend Zoe arrived at the library not long after the picture was posted and tried her best to comfort Kara while I just sat there, staring at my message from my faculty dean. He wants to see me, no doubt about this. I knew I would lose my job over this, but as I look at Kara, I can't help but feel terrible. She already feels bad enough about everything, especially about her mother, and I don't need to add this to her guilt.

"I have to go," I find myself saying anyway. I have to go meet him at some point.

"Why?" comes out Kara's soft voice. I smile at her, caressing her face with my hand.

"I have to take care of something, but I'll be back right after," I promise her. I'm going to try to not be away from her for any longer than I have to be.

I send her friend a look that says take care of her and she nods, sending me a thumbs up. I leave the library and walk to the dean's office, ignoring the stares I get from students and other professors on the way.

I take a deep breath before knocking on his door. I hear a soft 'come in' and with a bated breath, I walk in. He's sitting behind his desk, papers scattered all over the place with a frown creasing his face.

"I must say, I am disappointed in you, Professor Wilde," is the first thing he says. You've been working here for a significant while now, and I saw so much potential in you. Once I retired, I was going to suggest for you to take my place."

"I'm sorry," is all I can say.

"But love is love, isn't it?" he suddenly says, surprising me.

"Excuse me?" I say, unsure that I heard him correctly.

"I have a preposition for you. It may be a little unethical, but since Ms. Smith is a legal adult, it should be fine," he says.

"What is this preposition, sir?" I ask.

"You will quit your job, and then in a few years, once Ms. Smith has graduated, I will hire you back," he says. I must say, it's a pretty great offer, but the question still hangs in the air. Why?

"Why would you do that for me, sir?" I ask, unable to come up with a reason myself.

"I see myself in you, Professor Wilde," he says. "You have so much potential. It would be a real loss to lose you right now. But I'm willing to make that sacrifice for now, as long as you agree to return to the university once your...*lover* has graduated from her studies."

"Did you go through something similar?" I can't help but ask. He smiles.

"My wife, she too was my student once. In high school," he admits. "I know high school is different from university, but I think that this isn't so bad. Yes, Ms. Smith is young, but you're not like me. You are young too, with so much potential to prosper. I'm willing to give you the chance to."

"Then I don't see how I could say no," I say, and he breaks out into a smile.

"Then its settled," he says, clasping his hands together. "I wish you the best with your relationship, and I really hope it lasts."

I hope so too.

CHAPTER 32 – TAKARA

My mother is glaring at me.

After everything that happened, I dared to come home, knowing that she would be here, and now she's staring at me like she cannot believe I had the audacity to come here, after what I had done. She looks at me like I've stolen something precious from her, and well, I guess I did.

I don't know what part of me thought maybe she would accept things as they are, but it was clearly wrong. I should've known better than to get hopeful.

"Mom –"

"Don't," she cuts me off, holding a hand up in the air. "I can't-I can't even look at you right now."

She storms off and slams her bedroom door closed after her, causing me to jump slightly. My phone pings and I see Avery's name come up on the screen.

Ave <3: You okay?

I pull up my nose and type out a response.

Me: My mom hates me.

Ave <3: Oh, baby. I'm sure that's not true.

Me: She does!

Ave <3: No mother could hate her own child. Yes, your mother hasn't been the best mother, but she loves you. I'm sure of it. She's just hurt right now.

I know he's probably right. Doesn't make the way she looked at me hurt any less.

Ave <3: Do you want me to come pick you up?

I type yes, but I pause just before pressing send. Then I erase the text.

Me: No, I'm going to stay here. I need to talk to my mom.

Ave <3: Alright. Just let me know. I'm ready anytime for you.

I type a thank you before switching off the phone's screen. Then I sit down on the couch and wait.

I'm not sure how long I just sit there and wait until my mother finally emerges from her bedroom. She heads straight for the liquor cabinet and takes out a bottle of white wine.

"Mom," I call out, and she pauses her movements. "Can we-can we please talk?"

"I have nothing to say to you," she huffs like a little child.

"Good," I say. "Then you can listen."

She glares at my sass but doesn't move.

"Mom, I love Avery," I start off, and she flinches at my use of his first name. Yes mommy, he's no longer just Professor Wilde to me. "And he loves me. I'm really sorry that you're heartbroken right now and trust me when I say I know how it feels."

She purses her lips.

"I walked away from him once before, and it was literally the most miserable thing I ever put upon myself. So I won't do it again. I won't lose him again. I'm sorry if this hurts you, but he is *mine*, and just like I would have given him up for you should he have had feelings for you, you should too."

She blinks in surprise. Yes, mother. I'm no longer the selfish one here. So, don't be one either.

Mother doesn't say anything, but she puts the wine bottle back in the cabinet.

"Mom," I softly call out. "I love you."

She refuses to look at me, but that's okay. Even after everything, I still want her to know that.

"I love Avery."

I flinch at her words. Then she grabs the wine bottle again and glares at me.

"So if you decide to continue to be with him, you're disowned."

Tears fill my eyes.

Is she...is she really kicking me out? Disowning me? Over a man? But I'm her daughter...

"Mom –"

"Make a choice," Mother cuts in. I can't leave Avery again. I can't – Mother nods, finding my answer in my silence.

"I wish you well," is the last thing she says before disappearing back into her room. I sink back into the couch.

Then I send Avery a message.

Me: Come get me.

I'm done.

CHAPTER 33 – TAKARA

When Avery arrives, surprisingly, I'm not crying.

He loads my bags into the trunk of his car and then we're off. The entire drive to his apartment is quiet, him occasionally squeezing my thigh. When we arrive, I head straight to his bedroom and collapse onto the bed. He follows after me, climbing onto the bed and pulling me to him. He sits with his back against the headboard and I lay my head on his shoulder, letting him intertwine our fingers.

"She disowned me," I find myself telling him. He tenses. "She couldn't accept it. Us. So, she left me."

I sniffle slightly, feeling the tears come up. He hugs me tighter, rubbing the back of my head with his hand.

"I don't blame you," I tell him. "This was my decision too. I couldn't leave you."

"I wouldn't have let you either way," he admits and I find myself smiling.

"I love you," I mumble, placing my hand on his chest. He kisses the top of my head.

"I love you, too."

Somehow, hearing him say those three little words, heals all the hurt in my heart. That's how I know I made the right choice. If I had left him, I would be miserable, but now that I've chosen him, I'm happy. Content. At peace. I'm at home. With him.

Home is where he is. It's been for a while now, and now finally, it's just the two of us.

The two of us against the world.

But then our little bubble is burst by banging on the front door. Frowning, I sit up.

"Are you expecting anyone?" I ask, but he shakes his head. He gets up from the bed and I follow him to the front door. When he opens the door, a woman in her, I'm assuming thirties, bursts in, worry painted on her face.

When she sees me, she releases a breath, and then suddenly, she launches herself at me, enveloping me in a hug that nearly sends me falling back.

"I'm so glad you're here," she says, pulling back. "Are you okay? How are you feeling?"

I don't answer her, looking to Avery for answers.

"Chloe, you're overwhelming her," he merely says, shaking his head with a chuckle and closing the door.

"Oh!" Chloe says, before sending me a sorry look.

"Baby," Cameron calls out and I immediately gravitate towards him and into his awaiting arms. Chloe coos at the two of us. "Meet Chloe. My older sister."

Oh. She's his sister. The one he's always talked about. How did it not click in my brain, when they look so similar. Chloe is gorgeous, her eyes identical to Avery's, but has a head full of pin straight blonde hair.

"And you are Kara," Chloe says, taking a step towards me. "I've heard so much about you."

I nod, giving her a small smile.

"What are you doing here, sister?" Avery asks.

"You called. So I came," she simply says, giving him a confused look.

"Did you seriously leave your husband and child because of what I told you?" he asks, and she nods.

"You're my brother," she says, staring pointedly at him. "And you were in trouble. Of course I came."

"Did you...?" I trail off when he nods.

"Yes, I told her what happened," he confirms.

"And I was so worried," Chloe pouts. "But I'm glad to see you both are okay."

We both nod.

"Well, don't just stand there. Tell me everything," she demands. We all move to the living room, Avery and I sitting on one couch and Chloe on the opposite one. Then Avery proceeds to explain everything, including details about his work situation that he hasn't yet told me. For a moment, I feel guilty, but he reassures me that he's okay with it.

"Yeah, he can finally get a break, and besides. He has lots of money to keep him afloat for the next couple of years, and then more," Chloe says, offering me a comforting smile. I nod, grabbing onto his hand.

"Thank you," I tell him, and he squeezes my hand.

"Of course. You've sacrificed enough," he tells me, and I know he's talking about my mother, so I decide to tell Chloe about my mother and how she practically abandoned me.

"That bitch," Chloe curses, startling me. "Oh, oops. She's your mother after all. Sorry."

I shake my head.

"Its fine," I tell her. "She is a bitch."

Chloe bursts out laughing.

"I like you," she says. "I definitely like you."

I can't help but smile. Chloe, Avery's sister, the only living family he has, likes *me*. And so quickly. I'm relieved.

"You staying for dinner?" Avery changes the subject, but she shakes her head.

"I have to get going. I promised my husband I'd be home by tonight," she says with a smile. I love how she calls him her husband and not just by his name. I'd love to do that one day, with Avery, hopefully.

Chloe gives me and Avery one last hug, and then she's off, almost like she was never here.

"You okay?" Avery asks when she's gone. I nod.

"Your sister is funny," I tell him, and he shakes his head with a laugh.

"Why do I feel like you're going to like her more than you like me at the end of the day?" he grumbles, and I laugh.

"Don't worry," I say, cupping his face in my hands. "You will always be number one for me."

He smiles, leaning down and kissing me.

This is it. This is what I want.

Forever.

EPILOGUE – AVERY

My baby looks so beautiful.

In her graduation gown. With her graduation cap on her head.

She looks happy, too, as she accepts her diploma. Finally, after three long years, she's graduated. I cheer the loudest in the crowd, almost being overpowered by Chloe, but not quite yet. I'm the person most proud of her, and she needs to know that.

"She looks so pretty," Chloe gushes from beside me. Chloe has come to visit us a lot in the last three years and vice versa, and the two of them have become incredibly close, to the point that they hold secrets that Kara doesn't even tell me. Its fine, though, as long as she has someone to talk to.

"Professor Wilde," I hear someone call out, and I turn around, knowing that only one person still calls me professor. The history faculty dean smiles at me. "You're back."

I nod. I'm back.

He hands me a document before disappearing into the crowd. Chloe peeks over my shoulder.

"What is that?" she asks. I scan over the first page, the contents shocking me.

"It's an employee contract," I tell her. "But...it's not for a professor position. It's for the position of faculty dean."

Chloe gasps. Dean? I'm going to be dean?

"Ave!" I hear my baby yell out, but before I can look up to find her, she already collapses into my arms. "I graduated."

I laugh, wrapping my arms around her.

"Yes, you have. I'm so proud of you, baby."

She smiles, and then she notices the document in my hand.

"What is this?" she asks.

"Avery is going to be the dean!" Chloe exclaims, squealing so loud, everyone stares at us.

Kara goes quiet.

"You're going to be dean?" she asks softly, and I nod. Why? Is she not happy?

Then suddenly, she's throwing herself at me, wrapping her arms and legs around me and kissing me, not caring about the people that surround us.

"I'm so happy for you!" she exclaims, the brightest smile on her face. "You deserve this, Avery. You deserve it all."

I smile, kissing her again. Chloe cheers from beside us while Kara and I lose ourselves in each other.

This is it. This is all I've ever wanted. All I've ever needed.

And now I can finally say,

I have it all.

Also by Wie-aam Adams

Worldly Astray
Wanting Mr. Wilde

About the Author

I have lived my entire life Cape town, South Africa where my life is run by 2 furbabies, a husky named Saskya and a cat named Stripey. I'm a hopeless romantic who dreams of having the kind of love I read and write in books. Coffee and music are my writing companions. When not writing, I like creating art with my hands and paint tiny canvases. My sister has never let me live down THE oven incident. In my own defense, she asked me to turn the oven on, she did not ask me to set the temperature. My only secret, my obsessions are known by those who know me best, but even they don't know about my solo karaoke sessions.

Milton Keynes UK
Ingram Content Group UK Ltd.
UKHW040331310724
446271UK00019B/306